LYNNE TRUSS

The LUNAR CATS

arrow books

1 3 5 7 9 10 8 6 4 2

Arrow Books
20 Vauxhall Bridge Road
London SW1V 2SA

Arrow Books is part of the Penguin Random House group of companies whose addresses can be found at global.penguinrandomhouse.com.

First published by Century in 2016
First published in paperback by Arrow Books in 2017

www.penguin.co.uk

A CIP catalogue record for this book is available from the British Library.

ISBN 9781784756888

Typeset in India by Thomson Digital Pvt Ltd, Noida, India
Printed and bound in Great Britain by Clays Ltd, St Ives Plc

For Balls,
a cat who fell on his feet

Trade continues. Today the cat killd our bird M. Avida who had lived with us ever since the 29th of Septr intirely on the flies which he caught for himself; he was hearty and in high health so that probably he might have livd a great while longer had fate been more kind.

Joseph Banks, *Endeavour Journal*,
21 October 1768

Whether out of professional pique or some instinct of fear, the ship's mascot – a cat named Dowie, after Captain Turner's predecessor – fled the ship that night, for points unknown.

Erik Larson, *Dead Wake: The Last Crossing of the Lusitania*

Did things turn out well, generally speaking, Alec?

Yes, very well ☐ No ☐ Not really ☑ Don't ask ☐

Was anyone hurt?

Yes, very well ☐ No ☐ Not really ☐ Don't ask ☑

Has the world been rid of the evil cats?

Miraculously, yes ☑ Worryingly, no ☐ Too early to tell ☐

How do you feel about cats now?

Love them ☐ Indifferent ☐ Conflicted ☑ Hate them ☐

Cat Out of Hell

PROLOGUE

It is a moonlit night in eighteenth-century London. On to the shining cobbles in Wig and Gavel Yard bursts a group, buzzing with conversation and good cheer. They have clearly had a productive evening together. Yellow candlelight from the doorway strikes them dramatically from the side, and we can see tricorn hats, wigs and the odd clay pipe. The usual thing.

DR HAWKESWORTH

And so, gentlemen and lady, we are agreed?

All cheer.

DR HAWKESWORTH

Following the splendid paper on the Longitude Problem delivered to us this evening by Mr Timkins—

MR TIMKINS *bows, and is applauded merrily.*

DR HAWKESWORTH

—we, the London Lunar Society, on this evening of April sixteenth, 1768, sponsor Mr Timkins as our scientific representative aboard His Majesty's Ship *Endeavour!*

More cheering. Some miaowing. A bit of purring. But mostly cheering.

DR HAWKESWORTH

And now, may I propose that we end our evening in the traditional full-moon manner, gentlemen? May I call on our Italian friend Signor Andreotti to start us off?

SR ANDREOTTI

You may, sir. Ahem.

He adopts an operatic pose, with his tail stiff and vertical. Claws flexed. Whiskers shining in the dark. All fall silent. Indoors, someone snuffs out the candles, so that the darkness in the yard is better.

SR ANDREOTTI

(*yowling*)

Neeee-ooooOOOOWWW!

Then, one by one, they all join in, 'WaoooOOOW!', 'MiaoooOOWW!', until the sound of the yowling is quite loud.

Close-up on HAWKESWORTH, *who looks very pleased.*

Close-up on TIMKINS, *who looks excited but apprehensive.*

Aerial shot of the animated group lifts and widens to show the dark yard set amongst the alleys and narrow streets of eighteenth-century London, a pinpoint of nocturnal activity illuminated only by the moon.

Part One

Chapter One

If there is one thing I have learned from life, it is this: it is hard to know where a story truly starts. The present story, for example, has many beginnings from which to choose – but which was the real one? Was it, perhaps, the moment – on a recent dreary December morning – that I spotted the snippet of news in the *Daily Telegraph* concerning a spate of unexplained nocturnal 'abominations' in a far-off Bromley churchyard? I have the cutting before me as I write. Looking at this much-thumbed and badly tattered piece of newsprint with an unfortunate smear of lime marmalade in one corner (the tint is unmistakable),

I remember the decision to cut it out, and how I shivered at the time. But to be honest, I still shiver when I pick it up, and my breathing accelerates. This is partly at the remembered bitter temperature of that particular morning, which was unusually perishing. It is partly at the powerful (but quaint) word 'abominations' with all its high-flown biblical tone. But it is mainly, of course, at the recollection of the harrowing train of events that the Bromley churchyard story unarguably set in motion in my own life – events that are so heavily seared on my consciousness that they will attend me to my dying day.

At the time, however, I had no idea of its future significance, and I believe I actually said aloud, 'Oh, I've never been to Bromley in my life, have you?' – which is, I'm afraid, the sort of inane and pointless remark one makes when one lives alone; or alone with only a small and friendly dog for company, as I have done since the untimely death of my dear wife Mary three years ago. One makes such remarks not to the empty air (which would be mad, obviously) but, in my own case, specifically to Watson, as if I really believe that he understands every word I say. It's just a convention. It's a habit.

What can I tell you? It feels like talking. And while it's fair to assume that Watson does *not* understand every word I say, to his credit he usually gives a good impression of taking everything in. So I might say something inconsequential like 'I've never been to Bromley, have you?' and he looks up at me solemnly, from a sitting position, and behind those dark doggie brown eyes he seems, mentally, to be nodding his consent and admiring my sagacity. Of course, what he is actually doing – not only mentally, but with every element of his being – is feverishly counting the seconds until the clock hands tell me it's 5 p.m. (at last!), which is generally when his next unappetising doggie repast is due.

But perhaps you will already be familiar with Watson. After all, I have written about him before. More important for me at the present moment is not to introduce you to my charming dog, but to locate the true start of all that is to follow. Is the incendiary Bromley clipping the only candidate? Interestingly, it is not, because one might equally point to the strange anonymous email I received (around the same date, in that same week) from a secretive would-be maritime historian in Greece. I remember I had cleared some space on my untidy desk to put down an untidy mug of tea (everything in the house is untidy, I should explain), and I was about to search online for the number of a local framing shop when the email popped up, the sender's identity given as (unusual name) 'Thigmo Taxis'. It occurred to me that this unusual moniker was probably a pseudonym, but then I also had to admit that my knowledge of Greek names was quite limited, and that 'Thigmo' could actually be the first name of the current Greek prime minister for all I knew. So I tried not to be suspicious of Mr Taxis. I took a sip of tea and started to read what he had written. 'Dear Mr or Dr Delete as Applicable now Alec Charlesworth,' it began, and then it went on to make such a bizarre research request that I quite forgot about the tea.

Of late, I should explain, the 'Mr or Dr Delete as Applicable now Alec Charlesworth' so oddly addressed above (I am he) had of late been applying his dusty librarianship skills on behalf of professional authors. Some of these authors required help with research because they were 'hard pressed', I was told; but this was far from being the whole story. As soon became apparent, some were just shockingly lazy; others blithely uninterested in their own subject. All, I must report, were astoundingly ungrateful. But none of this made any difference to me. My new life began when my old assistant from the library found a job at a book publisher in London and became a 'contact': he recommended me to a well-known TV gardener hastily dashing off an account of the Napoleonic Wars, and I found the work (done mostly in the Cambridge university libraries, but also in London and on the Internet) both pleasant and intellectually rewarding, so eventually I advertised for more. My only complaint was that it seemed silly to hand over the material: why shouldn't I write the book itself? However, when I mentioned this feeling of frustration to my 'contact', he sternly warned me never to feel 'ownership of the material'. Naturally, I accepted this. But it was a real eye-opener, I have to say.

So, I was used to receiving requests for research. But I had never received an email quite like the one from Mr Taxis. First, there were the peculiarities in the form of address; second, there was no preamble about the book he was supposedly 'writing'; third, he did not explain how or where he had obtained my name and email address; and last, his request was highly specific. Thigmo wanted me to discover just one thing, as if to settle a bet: was there any evidence, he asked, connecting Dr Johnson's famous cat Hodge with the first Tahiti expedition of Captain Cook (1768–71)?

I sat back and laughed. Well, of course there would be no such evidence! What a ridiculous request! At first I ignored it. I found the number for the framer and made the call. I went to the untidy kitchen (down the untidy hall) and made another untidy cup of tea. Watson followed closely, of course, because he operates on the principle of sticking as close to me as possible, in case an old biscuit crumb should suddenly slip from my fingers, or a fragment of forgotten dog treat should fall from my pocket when I retrieve a hanky. So he followed me to the kitchen, and then followed me back again, with tail upraised and ready to wag, but not exactly wagging. I considered my options, in relation to Thigmo. A less scrupulous man would take the job, wouldn't he? He would write back, 'Be assured I shall put my very best team on this', and then he'd just stay indoors for a few days, with his feet up, rereading *The Moonstone*. Eventually he would write, 'No, I'm afraid after extensive research

I have found no evidence of Dr Johnson's cat being aboard the *Endeavour* on the voyage to Tahiti. That will be £1,500 plus photocopying charges.'

But, as it happens, I am quite a scrupulous man, so I did as much as a chap could do. I accepted the job. Over the next few days I consulted and searched all the accounts of the *Endeavour* voyage, looking for references to cats. I looked in the journals of Joseph Banks, the naturalist; in the three-volume *Account of the Voyages Undertaken by the Order of his Present Majesty for Making Discoveries in the Southern Hemisphere* by John Hawkesworth (1773); in Cook's own journals (as later printed); and in the account of Sydney Parkinson, one of the official artists on board, who tragically died on the return trip, aged only twenty-six, off the coast of Java. Wherever I looked for cats, I found nothing. But I enjoyed myself, and the idea of that great voyage through vast crystal seas certainly infiltrated my dreams at night – the small wooden world of the *Endeavour* pitching about on those deep Pacific waters, forging through the waves, navigating with such amazing Enlightenment accuracy towards the cartographical pinpoint of Matavai Bay in Tahiti. I heard the wind and the boom of the waves; felt the surge of the water below; the words of the old poem 'Drake's Drum' ('Captain, art thou sleeping there below?') kept running through my mind; as did, for some less literary reason, an image of Russell Crowe in a naval frock coat with his hair tied back in a ponytail.

You can tell from all this how ill-suited I am to the research business. I get much too involved. While other people were, annoyingly, on early Christmas shopping trips to London (and therefore getting in the way), I visited the National Maritime Museum at Greenwich and also the British Museum – just to look at some of the Pacific artefacts in the Enlightenment Gallery, brought back from the trip. The visit to the museum reminded me that I had once met an evil talking cat who claimed to have spent the whole of the Second World War there (*'I am proud to say that I know the layout of the Enlightenment Gallery better than I know the back of my own paw'*) – but I am getting ahead of myself here by mentioning an evil talking cat without preparing you first.

So how much did I learn about any connection between Hodge and the *Endeavour*? Precisely what I had expected to find: nothing. Not a thing. I noted (purely out of interest) that the *Endeavour* was itself a 'cat' – a type of coal ship, constructed in Whitby (and therefore known as a 'Whitby cat'). I also found that a later expedition to Tahiti released a small colony of cats on to the island, as a means of dealing with vermin, but they all seemingly disappeared. Sailors in the eighteenth century referred to a small local breeze that rippled the surface of the sea as a 'cat's paw'. A beam at the bow of the ship, used for raising the anchor, was known as the 'cat-head' – so that the anchor was said to be 'catted' when raised or secured. But whether there were actual feline cats on board with ears and claws and whiskers (and there surely must have been), not a single one of our eyewitnesses could be bothered to inform me.

Incidentally, to any modern reader accustomed to contemporary norms of travel writing, eighteenth-century sea journals are astonishingly disappointing. Wherever you expect a bit of 'colour', there is no colour. Where you expect a climax, there is no climax. Anecdotes are buried, punchlines never come; all dialogue is reported and flattened in the process. After months at sea, the ship reaches its destination, and you have to keep checking the dates of the entries to be sure that the momentous arrival has really taken place. No wonder all the journals were handed over to a professional writer (the humble John Hawkesworth aforementioned) – but poor Hawkesworth was at a disadvantage in several ways when it came to writing it up. First, he *hadn't been there himself*. And second, he was evidently an eighteenth-century landlubber essayist, accustomed to using a lot of abstract nouns, Latinate vocabulary, and costive constructions.

The most frustrating aspect of the first-hand accounts is that even if the decks of the *Endeavour* had been teeming with cats, none of these stolid eyewitnesses would have considered it of sufficient interest to mention. I felt guilty about Mr Taxis. I wished I could give him better news. And I also started to feel annoyed on his behalf, because of course there *must* have been cats aboard the *Endeavour*! All ships had cats – to keep the rats down, if nothing else. Everyone knows this. So why does no one mention them in these accounts? I know I have a suspicious nature, but I was beginning to think that the very absence of evidence for an *Endeavour* cat looked not only perverse but even a bit suspicious. Is it possible that mention of the presence of cats on this voyage was suppressed? The ship's artist, Sydney Parkinson (poor chap), helpfully compiled a glossary of Tahitian names for everyday things, including *ebapau* (a stool), *marama* (the moon) and *emahoo* (a turtle), and guess what? There is no word listed for cat! When I discovered this fact at the library, I was so annoyed that I had to shut the book and go for a walk round the reference section until I calmed down. I began to wish I'd taken the Wilkie-Collins-with-feet-up-that-will-be-£1,500 route instead.

At the same time as I pursued the Captain Cook line of enquiry, I also felt obliged to research the cat Hodge – looking for references beyond the much-repeated story in Boswell's *Life*, in which Johnson accidentally offends Hodge by saying that he has owned cats that he 'liked better' than this current one sitting on his lap. But there was nothing. What mainly struck me was how peculiar it is that this anecdote has become so well known. 'But he is a very fine cat, a very fine cat indeed' is often quoted out of context – inscribed on terracotta tiles and the like. I suppose what makes the story so memorable for cat lovers is that Johnson hastily corrected himself, 'as if perceiving Hodge to be out of countenance'. A statue of Hodge – generic cat, with oyster shells at his feet – now stands outside Johnson's house in Gough Square, off Fleet Street, in London. The oyster shells refer to Johnson's habit of feeding oysters to Hodge – which wasn't, in the eighteenth century, remotely on a par with decking it out in Prada accessories or providing it with its own account at Selfridges, but was still a mark of an owner's devoted care and affection. I can't help finding it odd, though, that this greatest of brainy men is almost best known not for his classical learning, epigrammatic wit, journalistic diligence and superhuman efforts with the *Dictionary*, but for – once, in front of witnesses – attempting to placate a huffy cat.

The research (if you can call it that) took me about ten days, and for good measure I included Johnson's well-recorded sayings on the nugatory value of travelling abroad. I have to confess I spent a lot of my allotted time just reading and rereading the email, and wondering about the person who had sent it. The wording was so odd, with unsettling repetitions, particularly of the often redundant word 'now'. 'Forgive the now far-fetched nature of this enquiry now,' it said. 'I would now be immensely grateful if now you can help me now.' There was something familiar here, but I couldn't put my finger on it. Given the Greek name, it was fair to assume that the sender was someone to whom English was a second language. But in what foreign language would the word 'now' be required for emphasis quite so frequently? Why would anyone hope to connect the cat Hodge with the voyages of Captain Cook in any case? Also – and I will explain later why this bothered me – why contact *me* in a matter concerning *clever cats*?

Clearly, both the Bromley news item and the Email of Nowness are candidates for the true start of my story, but I still can't be sure which one to choose. And there is (you will be unhappy to hear) yet a third candidate for the origin of all that follows – even though at the time it seemed the most inconsequential of events. Like the cutting in the newspaper, and the Hodge–Cook email, it occurred in dreary December. But instead of happening in my untidy house, it happened at the shops, in Poundland. I later referred to the incident as 'the fracas' – but I was so ashamed of it that I tried not to refer to it at all. Basically, I was shopping for novelty dog biscuits at a bargain price, for the simple reason that the amount charged for dog biscuits is criminal, and I had started to hyperventilate in fancy supermarkets whenever I saw the price labels on the shelves. So I decided to try my luck in a pound shop, fully aware that Mary would have warned me, 'You get what you pay for' – well, I certainly paid for these.

The last box of eight-sided 'Dogtagons' was on the shelf. It was marked (as of course you would expect, but it still impressed me) at *one pound.* I smartly took it down and put it in my basket, and was aware of a scream of rage as I did so; the next thing I knew, I was on the ground with a rather large woman on top of me. 'Give me those Dogtagons!' she was screaming. 'No!' I shouted back. 'Why should I?' The ensuing tussle was appalling. I thought she was going to bite me. No one came to my aid; in fact I noticed, as I thrashed about in fear of my life, that a couple of other shoppers had risen to the occasion only by backing off slightly to produce a better angle for filming me on their mobiles. Nor did the police automatically accept my story of the unprovoked assault: I was arrested for being part of an affray! I was asked how I could live with myself for fighting a woman over a pound's worth of dog biscuits! Luckily a CCTV camera had captured the whole thing – the way she rushed out of nowhere to knock me flat – and the woman remained in custody while I was allowed to go home.

'You might as well take these,' the policeman said, handing me the Dogtagons, which had accompanied us to the station.

'But I never got a chance to pay for them,' I objected.

The policeman rolled his eyes at my tiresome honesty. 'I'll pretend I didn't hear that,' he said.

When I returned home to Watson, I assumed that this ghastly episode could be put behind me, given time, but it ended even more quickly than I'd thought, because Watson rejected the Dogtagons out of hand; he sniffed them once or twice and walked off. So I threw them away. But of course it *didn't* end there, did it? Oh no. And my original point is well made, I think: you just never do know where a story properly starts.

So, to sum up, I had no idea, three weeks before Christmas, that yet again a great wave of a story was about to knock me down as I gratefully paddled through life's shallows with Watson at my side – knock me down and drag me into its churning depths! When I saw the item about the Bromley churchyard in the paper, it's true that I reacted with a flutter of excitement to the detail of an abnormally large cat sighted twice in the vicinity of the mysterious night-time excavations – because when I say that a great wave of a story might 'yet again' knock me over, I need to explain that three years previously I had been caught up in a terrifying (and improbable) series of events involving some cats – some evil talking cats, in fact, one of whom had spent the Second World War in the British Museum – and naturally there were times when I wondered (in a hopeful kind of way) whether the supernatural doings of the wonderfully sophisticated cat Roger and his huge cat-mentor, 'the Captain', were really at a positive end.

True, Watson and I had both witnessed the climactic joint death-plunge of Roger and the Captain down an old well in Dorset. (If I hadn't snatched Watson up in my arms at the last moment, he would have joined them down there.) We both knew for a fact that these two extraordinary cats – stripped of both their immortality and their powers by the selfless machinations of Roger – were gone for ever. The hair-raising events at snowy Harville Manor had provided a more-than-satisfactory conclusion to Roger's long and sorry life. And yet I'd retained for quite a while an optimistic reflex concerning cats. For at least a year, in fact, if I caught sight of any cat movement – a tail disturbing a bush; a feline leap, in the corner of my eye, from a car roof to a high wall – my pulse would race and I would think (and sometimes gasp aloud), 'Roger!'

Roger. Oh yes, Roger. It wasn't that I even knew him for very long. I think what made me fall in love with this beautiful cat was that I initially misjudged him so badly. You see, he alone had known the fate of a young woman, dying a horrible death in a cellar, and yet he had done nothing to save her. He had appeared to be in league with the Captain, who was a remorseless dealer of death; Roger seemed also to have engineered the horrible murder of a small terrier dog (a dog not unlike my own dear Watson). But as it turned out, Roger was the least evil of cats; he was blameless; he had even adored the dog! His entire goal for decades had been to avoid the influence of a demonic 'Cat Master' – and to narrate his own life story to a human being; but the Cat Master and the Captain between them had successfully thwarted (and terminated) his every friendship, with the effect that Roger's innocent course through life was littered with the corpses of the people who had loved him, and whom he himself had loved.

As you can imagine, a Grand Guignol experience involving demonic talking cats wasn't one I could drop casually into conversation with my Cambridge friends and neighbours. 'Dorset? Oh yes, what a charming county. Interestingly, I deliberately ran my car over an evil black cat in Dorset last winter but it did no good, of course, because he had been rendered immortal by having had nine lives already. The coastline is supposed to be very pretty, isn't it? But Watson and I didn't really see it, being a bit exhausted after witnessing a satanic ritual involving a deafening whirlwind indoors and a cat severing a major artery in a man's lap and then pumping all the blood out of him so that it spurted up like a geyser.' It was comforting that Watson had been through it all with me, but at the same time – well, you just never know with dogs how much they've taken in. Their intelligence is very different from ours. For example, they sometimes decide that the best course of action when confronted with a dangerous manifestation of a cloven-footed Beelzebub in a dark and empty Tudor house lit only by stubs of candles and with a pentagram chalked out on the floor is to bark at it and nip its hooves.

But if I couldn't exactly share the experience with Watson, I did emerge from the events with one natural confidant: an actor-chap named Will Caton-Pines (or 'Wiggy') – and although we had nothing otherwise in common, we felt bound to keep in touch. It was a relief for both of us that we could discuss those evil talking cats (or ETCs, as we afterwards called them, for short) with another human being. Wiggy had not only interviewed Roger extensively, he possessed recordings. Like me, however, he knew that his entire experience vis-à-vis the ETCs would be disbelieved by anyone neutral, especially if they had the extra qualification of being *not insane.* And what evidence did we have? The 'talking cat' of Wiggy's recordings could have been a fellow actor. With the physical entities of both Roger and the Captain gone for ever down a well, and with their so-called Cat Master shrivelled to unholy dust on the blood-spattered floor of Harville Manor (in Dorset), we both understood that we had only each other for support. It was just a shame (for me) that

Wiggy is a bit of an idiot, and that I have to take care what I tell him, because his imagination seems sometimes to operate well beyond his control.

To take the current instance, a few days after I had completed my Captain Cook research, I happened to write to Wiggy. Having nothing in my own life to tell him about, I told him about Johnson's cat; cats at sea in the eighteenth century; the Tahiti voyage; and so on. I even mentioned the interesting fact (gleaned from *Blackadder the Third*) that the word 'sausage' does not appear in Dr Johnson's *Dictionary*. All I wanted was for him to remember the incident; bookmark it, if you like, so that at a future date I might say, 'And you remember the email about Johnson's cat being aboard the *Endeavour*?' But no sooner has an idea gone into Wiggy's head than he must create something from it. In this case, he immediately consulted Wikipedia, and then dashed off a small scene in screenplay form, which I shan't include here, in case it derails my narrative. I will just say it is a major symptom of Wiggy's idiocy that he thinks he can write screenplays.

But the point is: were ETCs re-entering my life? When I started to suspect as much, the first thing I did was to check something. If you are familiar with my previous ETC adventure, you will know that I had in my possession a devilish pamphlet written by the penultimate 'Cat Master', an appalling man by the name of John Seeward. This pamphlet contained a list of Cat Masters, starting with Sir Isaac Newton in 1691. And I suppose I couldn't help wondering – what if Samuel Johnson's name was on this list? Naturally, I had not kept the pamphlet on display in my house. I had hidden it – hidden it rather cunningly, I thought. Anyway, when I retrieved it, I discovered that the list of Cat Masters was less complete than I had remembered. After the death of Newton (who invented the cat flap, did you know?), the post was taken first by Robert Walpole and then by the novelist and magistrate Henry Fielding; in 1754, after Fielding's death in Lisbon, it passed (until 1773) to a figure whose name is given only as 'the Adventurer'. I made a note, and hid the pamphlet again (it made me anxious to have it out in the open), and I considered the information. I was slightly disappointed, I admit. It didn't sound like Johnson. 'Adventurer' was hardly a name he would have chosen for himself – for his own publications, he chose less energetic epithets such as 'the Rambler' and 'the Idler'. The only 'Adventurer' in Johnson's career (I did investigate) appeared to be a short-lived literary magazine that he wrote for in the 1750s, which was surely not relevant.

I had just one clever thought concerning 'the Adventurer'. I decided not to tell Wiggy, in case he wrote another screenplay.

So to sum up, the story begins with one of the following:

1) abominations in a Bromley churchyard, as reported in the *Daily Telegraph*;

2) the email from a Greek man named Thigmo Taxis, asking me to research the putative maritime career of a cat embedded in 1760s literary London;

3) a fracas over some dog biscuits.

Oh, and I suppose I should mention one other thing. In that same week in December, another markworthy event:

4) a demon kitten came to live with us.

Chapter Two

The kitten was ginger and white, with pink ears and a pink nose and enormous eyes. Her name was Tetty. We heard her one night when I was putting out the recycling – a faint mewing from between the bins and the garden wall. It was a cold night, and I had intended a quick dash to the gate with a bag of thoughtfully rinsed milk cartons (I was wearing slippers with very thin soles), but I was stopped in my tracks. With the minimum of noise, I placed the milk cartons in the appropriate recycling bin, and then I just stood still. 'Hello?' I said – rather stupidly, as if the cat would say 'Hello' back (although this is not entirely without precedent, in my defence). I could feel the cold stone biting my feet through the slippers, but I tried hard not to move. 'Hello?' I repeated, and carefully shifted one of the bins aside, which caused a rustle of movement and a distinctive high-pitched mew. Gently does it, I thought. Don't scare the little thing. I heard the faint mew again. Now, if I reach *very* carefully into this dark corner, I thought, I might be able to—

But such calculations were pointless, because Watson – trotting out to join me, and catching on a little late – launched an immediate all-guns-blazing attack on the unknown intruder, barking and snapping, flushing out the tiny fluffball of a kitten, who made a great and screeching leap to escape him, and in a split second (I still can't put it together in my mind) some sort of heroic reflex made me catch her around the middle and grasp her to me, wriggling. Her reaction to being saved from Watson was, of course, to try to kill me. Cats are like this. Finding herself rescued, she bared her little sharp teeth; she hissed in my face, the heat of her breath making a cloud in the icy air. She also tore at my hands with her needle-sharp claws, so that they were soon deeply scored and bleeding. With Watson trying to jump up to reach her (despite my repeatedly commanding him not to), I held the kitten as high as I could (she was so *light!*) and watched her make frantic swimming motions while blood trickled down my hands and inside the sleeves of my jumper. 'Calm down,' I kept saying. 'Calm down, little cat. Calm down.'

I had a choice, I suppose. Given my special experience of cats, no one would have blamed me if I had set the kitten on the wall, said, 'Nice try, young demon puss,' and dragged the resisting Watson back inside. But I could too easily imagine what we would find the following morning: a frozen kitten, as stiff and lifeless as a plank, with its legs all sticking up in the air and its eyes wide open in goggling horror and pointed accusation. So I made my morally feeble decision. Much to the chagrin of the dog, I put the kitten under my arm (struggling) and carried her inside with us (still struggling), then I warmed it with a towel from the airing cupboard (struggling), quickly found an old shoebox for it to regard as its home (more struggling), and gave it some milk. At this point, she stopped struggling and fell instantly asleep, so I placed the shoebox on top of the boiler in the kitchen (very cosy for a cat) and set about placating Watson, who was – with good reason – both completely bewildered and extremely pissed off.

Now, I know what you are thinking. You are thinking that not since one Trojan said to another, 'Hey! An enormous horse statue thing has been sent to us by an anonymous admirer. We can't just leave it outside!' has anyone in a siege situation behaved quite so foolishly. Not since American pioneers were lured from the safety of their circled wagons by the sound (apparently) of human babies crying has such an obvious emotional trick been so easily pulled. All I can say is, you didn't see this kitten. Ginger and white, she was. Little pink nose. Soft as feathers to the touch. Big innocent eyes. A habit of holding her head on one side. And when she had calmed down, she was so responsive! One had only to stroke her lightly with the back of a (bloodied) finger and her whole being rose to meet the touch; her body arched; she purred like an engine; her head pushed strongly against one's (lacerated) palm.

There being no collar, I decided to give her a name. Again you will be shrieking at me that I am an idiot, and that I should have done less in the christening line, more in the fur-examination line, looking for the giveaway numbers 666 indelibly tattooed on the skin. 'Put her out in the snow! Are you mad?' But I am a verbal person, I'm sorry, and I wanted the kitten to have a name. Even if she turned out already to have a home elsewhere (I would have to advertise in the morning), I wanted her to have a name while she lived with me. So, while she slept, I stroked her head and pondered the question of what would be suitable. I looked round the kitchen for inspiration – and that's how I settled on 'Tetty'. The books from my recent research into Dr Johnson and the South Seas still littered the kitchen table: not a single female person appeared in any of these voyage accounts, but I suddenly remembered that 'Tetty' was Johnson's pet name for his wife, Elizabeth, and it struck me as a very pretty name for a very pretty girl.

Watson remained incensed about the kitten. He gave me a lot of meaningful looks. I couldn't blame him. In fact, I kept apologising to him when we were alone. I gave him special biscuits by way of compensation. Wiggy, on the other hand, was very excited. I called him the next morning, from

Watson's walk. As I have mentioned before, Wiggy was my only choice of confidant in such matters.

'Now the thing is, Wiggy, we mustn't get carried away,' I said. 'There is always the possibility that this is *just a kitten*.'

Wiggy wasn't listening. He had gone instantly into Code Red mode. 'You must behave totally normally, Alec,' he said. 'She mustn't know you suspect. Have you indicated in any way that you suspect? Think, Alec. Think.'

'I'm not sure I do suspect, Wiggy. That's the problem.'

'Are you joking? A cat wheedles its way into your house and you're not suspicious? You just called me, didn't you? Why did you do that if you don't suspect?'

'But not every cat is an evil talking cat!'

'Or an ETC,' he pointed out. (He liked to use the shorthand terminology wherever possible, and this was a Code Red, for heaven's sake. Why invent these special abbreviations if we didn't use them now?)

'Or even an ETC,' I agreed. 'I'm trying to keep a level head, that's all. This kitten is only about eight weeks old. Millions and millions of cats are *not* ETCs.'

'But those millions and millions are not in your house!'

'I know. Yes, you're right.'

'This one is in your house, Alec.'

'Right. Yes. She is, yes.'

'So, you're saying you haven't actually heard the kitten speak yet?'

'Of course I haven't!'

'Not even a casual "good morning"?'

'No. No, it's all perfectly normal. A bit of miaowing. Some purring. A lot of surprisingly violent slashing and ripping of skin. Also, she's torn one of Watson's toys to bits. He'd had it since he was a puppy—'

'I've had a thought,' he interrupted.

'Go on.'

'You could just say "Good luck" to her. When she's off her guard, you see. And then she might say, sort of without thinking, "Thank you."'

'I could,' I said, in a measured way, wondering why this particular ploy sounded familiar. 'Like in *The Great Escape*?' I said at last.

'Exactly! Like in *The Great Escape*.'

I didn't want to argue. 'OK,' I said. 'I'll try that.'

'And you haven't caught it reading the paper or anything?'

'She only arrived last night!'

Wiggy considered this. 'I'm still trying to take it in, Alec. I mean, is there no end to their evil? The very idea of an evil *kitten*! An ET*K*!'

'Unless it's just a sweet little lost kitten. Or an SLLK.'

Wiggy sighed. 'Right,' he said uncertainly. He changed the subject. 'How's Watson?' he said.

'Oh, well, he's furious.'

'I'm not surprised. You didn't leave him on his own with her?'

'Good God, no. He's with me now.'

'Oh, good.'

I didn't know what else to say. Watson stopped for a copious wee against a favourite tree. I bit my lip. The reason I had called Wiggy – it wasn't just that I felt I should share some suspicions. In the weeks after the events at Harville Manor, we had put in place a few precautions. It had been Wiggy's idea, mostly. 'Plan Cat Intruder', he called it (or 'PCI'). Basically, we had bought tiny surveillance cameras for our homes, and we had made solemn (though unnecessary) promises never to spy on each other except when Plan Cat Intruder was jointly invoked. Was this the right time to bring the PCI into play? I wasn't sure. I decided I wouldn't be the first to mention it. Tetty was a tiny feeble creature whose eyes had just learned to focus, and whose little head bounced delightfully against the cupped (injured) palm of my hand when I stroked her. She was just a kitten!

'Did you leave the cameras on?' he said.

What a relief!

'I did, yes,' I said. Then hesitantly, 'But are you sure this is really the right time to—'

Wiggy interrupted. 'Of course it is. Are you crazy?'

'Oh, go on then. Do you remember how to access them?'

'Absolutely. Doing it now.'

I was pleased. I also felt quite excited. Why I *wanted* the kitten in my house to be of a demonic disposition, I can't explain. But I did. If this kitten simply grew up to become a boring, standard house cat, I'd be thoroughly disappointed; I might also be lumbered for life with an animal who reserved the right to slice my living flesh into strips whenever it felt like it, and also (sorry to mention this) do its poo functions inside the house, in a smelly box of gravel. Watson and I had reached the little parade of shops where I usually bought my newspaper; since Jay (the newsagent) was famously generous with dog treats, Watson was far from happy that we had mysteriously stopped short and that I was now lost in a phone call. He tugged at the lead. I told him to be patient. He attempted a growl and I told him to stop it. Meanwhile, down the line, I could hear the tap of a keyboard, with accompanying Wiggy mutterings of 'Oh, come on' and 'Not that one' – until, finally, 'Here we are.'

'I left her in the kitchen,' I said.

'Kitchen, kitchen,' said Wiggy to himself, tapping keys. 'Crikey, Alec, your living room! It's really untidy!'

'I know,' I said. 'I didn't ask for you to—'

'That looks like a health risk, Alec, if you don't mind my saying so. I mean, rule number one is that you should at least be able to see the floor.'

'It's not that bad when you're in it,' I said defensively. 'It's just cosy.'

'It's a *mess*,' Wiggy said. But he was still tapping keys, so I let it go.

'Kitchen!' he said at last. Watson tugged at the lead, and I tugged back. I switched the phone to the other ear.

Wiggy tapped the keys some more, and then gasped.

'Right. Can you see her?' I said.

But there was only silence, with breathing.

'What's happening?' I said.

'Oh my *God*,' he said, in a drawn-out kind of way.

I held my breath. What was he seeing? 'What is it?' I said. What had the kitten done? What evil had she already wrought while my back was turned?

'Oh my *Gaaawd!*'

'What? What's she done?'

'Oh, Alec,' he whispered.

'*What?*' I said.

'You didn't say she was so gorgeous!'

I sighed. This is the problem with working with Wiggy.

'I know that, thank you! I know she's gorgeous. But what's she doing?'

'She's so tiny.'

'I know.'

'That little nose!'

'I know. She's adorable. But what's she doing?'

'Sorry?'

'What's she doing, Alec? Is she obviously casing the joint? Opening cupboards? Are her lips moving? Is she *reading*?'

'Oh. No. No, no, no. She's just licking herself.'

'That's it?'

'That's it. She's on top of the boiler, on a cushion. Licking herself.'

'Like a kitten, in fact?'

'Yes. Like a kitten.'

I sighed. 'I'm sorry, Wiggy. Forget I called. It's just that there was that funny email from Greece, and that piece in the paper about the cat digging in Bromley, and that attack in Poundland, so I've been feeling a bit like something is happening, but I don't know what. But Tetty's just a kitten. She's just a normal kitten.'

There was no reply. Just heavy breathing, and more tapping. He was perhaps getting a close-up of the kitten's adorable little ears.

'Wiggy?'

'Mm?'

This was getting annoying. I was cold. Watson wanted to go. I wished I'd dressed him in his special fleecy coat.

'I was just saying—'

'Sorry, Alec. What did you say?'

'I said, forget I called. I was over-reacting. I'm sorry.'

He tried to escape the fascinating pull of the gorgeous kitten. He tried to remember that this might be serious.

'She's only just inveigled her way into the house, Alec. She might still be working out a plan of action.'

'Or she might just be a kitten!'

He sighed. He was (if I may risk a rhyme) smitten (with the kitten). Eventually, he said, dreamily, 'Yes.'

We both had a little think.

'She does *look* like she's just a kitten, Alec.'

'I know.'

'I can see why you'd have suspicions about her being the latest manifestation of timeless Cat Evil – but oh, look, oh, bless her, she's *yawning!*'

The next few days were difficult. England was being battered by wind and rain; the high street chains were complaining that Christmas custom was slow to build (because everyone was sensibly staying indoors); unprecedented flooding was the main item on the news; the sun went unseen for days on end. Indoors, we had the lights on all day. I was cosy enough, but very confused. Half the time I was monitoring the kitten and trying to trick it into giving itself away; the rest of the time I was admonishing myself for being so ridiculous, and just adoring her. (As you can see, I couldn't settle on a pronoun, either. The kitten was an 'it' when I was suspicious, but she was a 'she' whenever I acknowledged how lovable she was.) One very obvious option was open to me: take the kitten to an animal shelter. Be rid of her. But I couldn't bear to do that. It is amazing how, in life, we can sometimes entertain two opposite beliefs. If you had asked me, during the days that Tetty spent with us, whether I believed she was an immortal, cold-hearted agent of Cat Evil in kitten form, or whether I believed, conversely, that she was a totally innocent, warm-blooded kitten joyfully experiencing everything for the first time in her tiny young life, I'd have said without hesitation that I believed both things. Tetty was a gorgeous kitten. When I half-heartedly opened a box of old Christmas decorations one afternoon, she jumped into it and rolled about, getting herself adorably tangled in some tinsel! When I watched TV, she lay on my lap with her legs in the air. But was she just pretending not to be interested in what was happening on screen? I had no idea. As I stroked her, I could sometimes feel the quickening of her pulse in response to bits of information. When I deliberately watched wildlife programmes (especially anything about cats), she would squirm under my hand. In one programme monitoring cat territories in a suburban neighbourhood, Tetty first got hot to the touch, then twitched and fidgeted, and finally she sat back on her haunches and – looking me in the eye – raised a paw and deliberately slashed my leg.

I tried quite hard to trick her into speaking. While she was in residence, I watched only films notable for twists and surprises, hoping she wouldn't be able to control herself when the narrative bombshell was dropped. I fully expected her first words to be an exasperated 'What? So Keyser Söze *doesn't exist*?' I would start nursery rhymes and then stop abruptly before the end ('Old MacDonald had a—'), hoping she would step in and finish them. I left around books such as Paul Gallico's *The Silent Miaow* and Desmond Morris's *Catwatching*, hoping to catch her engrossed in reading. I even tried saying 'Good luck' in a casual sort of way (and in a German accent), in the hopes she would reply, unthinkingly, 'Thank you very much.' But were we having a battle of wills here, or was I just insane? Wiggy suggested I go down the cryptic crossword route (during the time he'd lived with Roger, he used to cut out the *Telegraph* crossword for Roger every day). So I started doing a book of crosswords in a slow, annoying, thinking-out-loud sort of way, and sometimes Tetty jumped up on the table and sat at my elbow, looking alternately up to my face and down to the puzzle, up and down, up and down, as I attempted (apparently) to solve the cryptic clues.

'Oh, I can't get this, little Tetty,' I said one darkened afternoon. 'Look, the clue is "Cutting cards? No, I shuffled (8)", and when I looked up the answer it's "sardonic". How on earth do you get that? What's that got to do with card-cutting?'

I stared at the clue, as if in despair. (In fact, it's quite easy. 'Sardonic' is another word for 'cutting', and you can make it by rearranging – or 'shuffling' – the letters in 'cards' and 'No, I'.)

Tetty blinked a few times, as if processing something. She looked up at me quizzically.

'Perhaps it's an anagram of "shuffling",' I said, and then I laid out all the letters, S, H, U F, F, L, I, N, G, in random order, in a rough circle. Then, after staring at them for about two minutes, I crossed them out again. 'No, no, that can't be right. There's no "g" in sardonic!'

All this pantomime definitely held her attention. Tetty looked down at the clue, and looked back up at me as if horrified. *You can't get this?* was definitely her kittenish expression.

'If only I knew what sardonic meant,' I shrugged. 'I suppose that would help!'

Tetty put a paw on the back of my hand and searched my face. She sniffed me. She knew I was lying. But if she knew I was lying, she also knew why I was doing it.

'Oh heavens!' I exclaimed suddenly. 'What time is it?'

Tetty's eyes went straight to the clock on the cooker.

'It's half past four,' I said. 'Nearly your teatime.'

She purred and rolled on to her back, so that I could see (but definitely not touch) her furry little tum. She mewed attractively. She knew she had made a mistake by looking at the clock.

I lifted her down to the floor and said, 'And after tea, we're going to watch a movie called *The Sixth Sense.*'

The only time I didn't lay traps for Tetty was during quiz shows – so it was ironic that a quiz show provided the one solid piece of evidence as to her true abilities. On *Pointless* one afternoon, the question consisted of five photographs of 1950s British stars, and I rattled them off contentedly – 'Diana Dors, Norman Wisdom, Dirk Bogarde, Dennis Price, Alec Guinness' – and then I was just deciding that the best answer (as the most obscure) was Dennis Price, when the kitten looked up and blurted, 'Dirk bleeding Bogarde? Laurence Harvey more like.'

'Who did she sound like?' asked Wiggy the next morning. And I was pleased he asked, because I had been pondering this all night, and had finally reached a conclusion.

'Barbara Windsor,' I said.

He laughed. 'What, cockney?'

'Cockney, rough, but still feminine, and with a distinctly comedic inflection.'

I had texted Wiggy the next morning and we had agreed to meet. I'm not sure if I've mentioned that we both live in Cambridge. We met at Parker's Piece. For the first time in a week, it wasn't raining.

'I wonder what she's after,' said Wiggy.

'I don't know.'

'Where's the pamphlet?'

'What?'

'Where's Seeward's pamphlet?'

'It's in the cereals cupboard. It's quite safe. Behind the Fruit 'n Fibre. She could never get in there. She's too little. How on earth does she know the difference between Dirk Bogarde and Laurence Harvey? It's quite annoying, actually. I'd been trying everything. We watched all of *The Others* on Saturday night and when it turned out it was Nicole Kidman who was the ghost, I was completely flabbergasted but Tetty didn't bat an eyelid.'

'Has she ever seen you with the pamphlet?'

He was right to keep harping on about the pamphlet. After all, people had died for it in the past, my dear wife Mary being one of them. I suddenly wondered whether I should just have destroyed this incendiary document, rather than mixing it in with the muesli and hoping for the best. But in my defence, I thought all the evil cats (all the ETCs) were no longer around to require it. With the demise of the last ever Cat Master (Julian Prideaux) on that spectacular night in Dorset three winters ago, the whole ancient cult of the Nine Lives had surely come to an end. Prideaux had named no successor; he had also been slain by one of his own cat protégés. There could be no more Cat Masters; no more 'nine lives' initiations, where cats suffered eight deaths to emerge as immortal uber-cats like Roger and the Captain. The mysteries recorded for posterity by John Seeward in the *Nine Lives* pamphlet were now, therefore, of nothing but academic interest. There was just one small memory niggling me: that when Roger was asked (by me) what the experiments at Harville had been in aid of, he had refused to say. I had said, 'What did happen here?' and Roger had replied, with a catch in his voice, 'Oh Alec, you don't want to know. All I can say is that it involved . . .' and here he had found it hard to speak, 'it involved *kittens*.'

'Sorry, what was the question?'

'Has the kitten ever seen you with the pamphlet?'

'Right. Well. No. No, I don't think so. The last time I looked at it was to check the list of Cat Masters—'

'To see if one was Dr Johnson?'

'That's right.'

'That was when she turned up, wasn't it?'

'Oh, yes.'

I called to Watson, who was off the lead and leaping up to catch a Frisbee that definitely didn't belong to him. I harrumphed. A woman with a poodle was shouting at him. I joined in:

'Watson! No!'

He ignored me.

'Drop it! Watson! Drop it!'

This made no impact.

'Drop it! Drop it! I said, DROP IT!'

But Watson did not drop it. I'm always having to apologise for him for things like this. Instead of dropping the Frisbee, he was now shaking it viciously, as if trying to break its neck.

'So who *was* the Cat Master, then?' asked Wiggy. 'If it wasn't Johnson?'

And I said, shiftily, 'Ooh, I can't remember.'

I set off to collect Watson, suddenly aware that since the kitten had arrived in the house, I had let a lot of things go. It was not only the identity of the 'Adventurer' that I'd neglected to follow up; there had been more stories about the churchyard in Bromley, too. But I had given no thought to them, being transfixed by the way Tetty curled up in the crook of my arm and rested her head (so lightly!) on my forearm. Meanwhile I'd had several urgent follow-up emails from Mr Taxis in Greece demanding that I dig deeper for evidence of cats on the *Endeavour*, and even directing me to look at a particular passage in Joseph Banks's *Journal* for October 1768; again, I had instead helped the kitten down from the dining-room curtains, where she had – so helplessly! – got her claws caught in the fabric. I had also received a letter of apology from the woman who'd attacked me in the pound shop; and I'd done nothing about that, either, because on that day Tetty had been 'digging' in the sofa, and had pulled out quite a lot of horsehair. The eccentric Poundland attacker had bizarrely enclosed a packet of high-quality dog biscuits (already opened, I noticed), by way of making amends. Legally speaking, she should never have been in touch. But what worried me more – though only fleetingly – was that she knew what my name was and where I lived.

We walked on. I suggested that Wiggy come home and meet the kitten, but he decided against it. He was worried that it might make the kitten suspicious (which was quite a good point). He was also worried he might say something stupid in front of the kitten and give the game away (unfortunately, ditto).

'How about a trip to Bromley?' he said. 'You know they're talking about this one huge, powerful cat now?'

'Are they?'

'Yes. Reading between the lines, it might have dug up a *whole body*.'

He said all this with suitable feeling, but still I failed to take it in. A cat had *dug up a body*? In *Bromley*? For some reason, I only thought of the distance from Cambridge to Kent, especially if one were making the journey in the week before Christmas with a pissed-off doggie at one's side.

That afternoon, with all the lights on and the kitten asleep in her box in the kitchen, I decided to consult the Internet on the subject of Bromley churchyard. The news stories from the broadsheets and websites were sparse in detail. There had been sightings of a sort of Beast of Bodmin (predictably christened the Beast of Bromley). Locals had given statements about seeing a huge cat in the churchyard at night; there was a picture of large, fresh claw marks on the oak doors of the church, which awakened some pretty awful memories in me. Why had I not been taking this story seriously? I can only say that the kitten had distracted me; but also, I do need to say this: I'm not an official Catfinder General or anything. I never actually volunteered to rid the world of evil talking cats! I am a retired academic librarian, with a civil service pension, a sideline in research, and a penchant for watching, and rewatching, old Hercule Poirot dramatisations on ITV3 in the afternoons. I am averse to danger. I am ambivalent about cats. I have never been remotely attracted to the supernatural. So I think it's quite reasonable to ask: *why me?*

But I do get hooked by a story, I suppose. Which is why I was now discovering online that the parish church at Bromley (St Peter and St Paul's) had ancient origins, but had suffered serious bomb damage during the Second World

War, when only its tower survived. The urgent question was: who was buried there? Well, no one of any great importance, evidently. The Kent Archaeological Society website gave a list of more than eight hundred names, though, and I gratefully printed it out, to consult later. Scanning it, I noticed a number of Youngs, Tweedys and Thornhills. What had caught my eye was a piece of local BBC news from a week before. It was almost a throwaway item – a little vox pop conducted on the streets of Bromley, with everyone damp and windswept, the reporter manifestly resenting this absurd assignment (with rain speckling his glasses), and the wind loudly buffeting the microphone.

'Are you worried about the so-called Beast of Bromley?' he asked a young woman with too much make-up and exaggerated streaking in her hair, whose straining umbrella was threatening to lift her off the ground.

'Nah,' she said. 'No one I know's seen it. It's an urban myth.' She was obviously quite proud of knowing this expression. The umbrella rattled and whistled like a mainsail in a typhoon. She was holding it down with an effort that showed in her face and voice. 'That's what we think. It's an urban myth.'

Two elderly shoppers in a bus shelter said that this was nothing to worry about; reports of rogue cats around Bromley had been 'going the rounds' since before the Second World War! This was nothing new, they said. Oh yes, these stories 'went the rounds' every so often, and this story was 'going the rounds' again now.

A young couple took it a bit more seriously. They had a baby in a sling. The young man (with a face tattoo) said he didn't know what to make of the Beast of Bromley, but what he did know was that the family cat had disappeared. 'He just went,' he said. 'It was like he heard a call.'

His partner said, 'But he's done that before.'

And the man said, 'Yeah, but he's always come back before, babe, and he hasn't this time, has he?'

The reporter asked him, 'What do you mean, "it was like he heard a call"?'

The man shrugged. His face tattoo shrugged with him. 'Well, he just sort of sat up and listened, and then he ran off.'

A little boy made a lion face and roared into the camera, while his parents laughed indulgently.

This childish failure to take the story seriously made me huff with impatience.

Finally, a middle-aged policeman in a peaked cap, speaking under lights while illuminated rain swirled behind him, assured the public that there was no 'beast' at work, but that the police were treating the mysterious excavations in the graveyard extremely seriously, and examining evidence.

While he was talking, we saw a shot of the churchyard in flat daylight (presumably filmed earlier in the day) with incident tape fluttering from metal stakes that had been stuck in the grass. Beyond, there were evident disturbances in the earth.

Then the reporter summed up straight to camera, with a melee of camera-curious shoppers behind him, all hanging on to their umbrellas with grim British determination. The people of Bromley, he said, were not unduly alarmed; he wasn't much alarmed himself; he just hoped that nice young couple's cat would come back for Christmas! And back to the studio, where the attractive regional anchorperson was smiling brightly, although behind her eyes (as usual) you could see an unhappy brain quite clearly thinking: I'm better than this.

I watched this diverting news item twice before I spotted her. In the introductory shot and in the last one – the two that were filmed on the streets – there she was. The woman who had attacked me in Poundland. I scanned forward; I scanned back; I freeze-framed. It was her. A stocky woman with a prominent chin and practical brown shoes and a brown woollen hat. I suddenly remembered the weight of her body and also the smell that had come from her – a mixture of meat stew, incense, and Parma violets. What was the name of this woman? I had left the letter on the kitchen table with the unwanted packet of dog treats, so I now opened the kitchen door and was so confused by the scene I discovered that it took me a moment to take it in. Because as I pushed the door open, my eye travelled immediately to little Watson, who appeared to be staggering about. This was strange. He was also panting heavily. And on the floor there was a mess of crumbs and biscuits and something liquid and lumpy that looked like vomit.

'What's up, doggie?' I said in a normal tone.

He responded by panting and staggering to his left.

It was only now that I realised something was wrong. 'Watson?' I said.

Watson spewed on the floor – a white, paste-like spew, like ectoplasm – and staggered again.

'Oh my God. Watson!' I cried. Had he been poisoned? But how? He hadn't left the house!

It was then that I noticed the kitten was standing on the table with the overturned packet beside her. The packet that the mad old Poundland woman had sent. The kitten had knocked the biscuits on to the floor.

'Tetty?' I said.

At which she looked straight at me, then waved a paw over the scattered biscuits and said, 'Ooh, my stars. Look at that! I'm ever so sorry, dearie.'

The next few moments were a blur as I picked up Watson, wrapped him in my best jacket (it was on the back of a chair) and grabbed my car keys. But I'll never forget how Tetty looked at me – so steadily, so *challengingly*, while I hastily pocketed my mobile phone, holding the suffering doggie under my arm. Didn't she care *at all*? My abiding memory is that, while I was in such distress, while Watson was fighting for breath, Tetty sat down on the tabletop, lifted a furry back leg and licked it.

'What have you done?' I said. 'You fiend!'

I wish I *hadn't* said 'You fiend', by the way, but I've noticed before how it's hard to be original *in extremis.* I shut the kitchen door on the kitten and I locked it from the outside before dashing to the car. I put Watson in the back seat and called the vet to say I was bringing him in. The receptionist told me to make him drink some water, but I explained we were already on our way. It was a terrible journey. Watson kept vomiting, which I assumed was a good thing (although not for my jacket); but the traffic was slow and I was going out of my mind. When we finally arrived at the surgery, Watson was taken straight from my arms and I'm ashamed to say I went to pieces in the waiting room the moment it was convenient to do so. A well-dressed woman with a tabby cat in a basket and a foreign man with a Pomeranian, whose appointments I had just hijacked, sat awkwardly looking at the floor (or whispering words of comfort to their pets) while I snivelled in my shirtsleeves, and then gave way to sobs. Even when the nurse came out of the consulting room and told me that Watson was going to be fine, I couldn't stop. In fact, the news that he would survive, after all, made me sob and snivel all the harder.

'That's good,' said the cat woman, sweetly. She patted me on the arm, and I struggled to say something, but couldn't. 'Are you warm enough?' she asked.

I wasn't. But I couldn't see the point of talking about it.

'He looked like a nice dog,' said the Pomeranian man.

'He is!' I wailed. I remembered shouting at him in the morning for his perpetual purloining of other dogs' Frisbees; why, oh why was I such a heartless disciplinarian?

'Gabrielle was poisoned once; I know what it feels like,' said the cat lady, indicating the basket. I looked in at Gabrielle. She looked back at me with murder in her eyes.

In the end, the vet said she would keep Watson for the night. I could go home. They were sure he'd be better by the morning.

'But you got him here just in time; it was a potentially fatal dose,' she said brightly, assuming this would cheer me up – instead of which I broke down again, at the thought of what might have been if I had sat at my computer, gazing at the mysterious Bromley woman, just a couple of minutes longer.

It was only when I was back outside in the cold fresh air that I realised I was scared to go home. What on earth should I do about the kitten now? 'Ever so sorry, dearie,' it had said. 'Ooh, my stars.' It had shown its paw, in no uncertain terms; it was also somehow in cahoots with the Poundland attacker! I kept remembering my melodramatic denouncement – 'You fiend!' – which made me shrivel with embarrassment. And yet it wasn't far from the mark. The only thing that would make such a fiendish kitten even more of a danger to humanity would be if it possessed the *Nine Lives* pamphlet, which I had so stupidly retained in the house. Scared or not, I must get home as soon as possible! I must also get a jumper or a coat on, fairly soon, as I was freezing.

My phone rang as I was opening the front door to the house. I checked the ID. It was Wiggy.

'Oh, go away, Wiggy – not now!' I said as I pressed 'Deny'. But as I was about to unlock the kitchen door, the phone rang again.

I took a deep breath and answered it, the unturned key still in my hand.

'Wiggy!' I panted. 'This isn't the best time! Watson's been poisoned! And Tetty did it.'

'Oh Alec.'

'So I'm in a bit of a state, as you can imagine.'

'Of course. I'll ring you back.'

'It's not important?'

'No, no. Poor Watson, is he going to be OK?'

'They think so.'

'I'm glad.'

I started to turn the key in the lock. 'So I have to deal with Tetty now,' I said, which reminded Wiggy of why he had called.

'Ooh, well, that's the thing,' he said. 'I thought I ought to warn you.'

I opened the kitchen door. A strong aroma of meat stew and Parma violets hit me as I entered the room, but tragically I failed to apprehend its significance.

'Warn me?' I said.

'Yes,' he said. 'I thought I should warn you: don't go home.'

The kitchen had been ransacked. Table and chairs overturned; drawers disturbed; fridge pulled out. Even a person whose untidiness sometimes draws hurtful comment from their closest friends could see that this kitchen was in a terrible state. Someone had evidently been looking for something – and it was someone with a lot more muscle than an eight-week-old kitten. The cereal cupboard, unsurprisingly, had not been spared. A lot of Fruit 'n Fibre had been broadcast around the room; a dusty layer of muesli and porridge oats was over every surface.

I stepped further into the room.

'Oh no!' said Wiggy at once.

'What?' I said. 'What's happened?'

'No, it's you,' he said. 'I'm watching on the cameras, and you're there!'

'I know I'm here. What happened here?'

'You went home!'

'I know I went home. I'm here now. What are you trying to tell me?'

'Oh, look out, Alec! Look out!'

At which point I was struck from behind. And as Philip Marlowe might have put it (but luckily, never had cause to), a pool of Quaker Oats opened up in front of me, and I dived in.

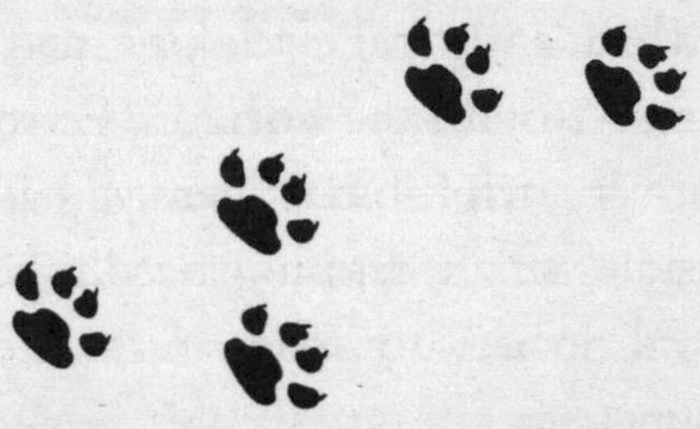

Crossing the Equator

On Tuesday, 25 October 1768, the *Endeavour* crossed the equator. Using all my nautical knowledge, I can tell you the ship was somewhere in the Atlantic, having headed south from Madeira, and that it had caught a helpful breeze. I am grateful to Mr Thigmo Taxis for directing me to the relevant section of Banks's *Journal.* Here, for the purposes of comparison, are the various (and considerably different) accounts that have come down to us of that noteworthy day.

(An 'azimuth', by the way (I've just looked it up), is the direction of a celestial object from the observer, expressed as the angular distance from the north or south point of the horizon to the point at which a vertical circle passing through the object intersects with the horizon. Personally, I don't find that very helpful, but there you are. Cook's 'Deping Needle' was a dipping needle lent to him by the Royal Society to assist in investigating the earth's magnetism.)

JAMES COOK: *JOURNALS*

Tuesday 25th. Winds SE to SEBE. Course S 30° W. Distce in miles 95. Latd in 0°15' South. Longd in West from Greenwich 29°30'. Bearings at Noon Do N 26° E Dt 358 leagues.

A Gentle breeze and clear weather, with a moist air. Soon after sun Rise found the Variation of the Compass to be 2°24' West being the mean result of several very good Azimuths, this was just before we crossed the line in Longitude of 29°29' West from Greenwich. We also try'd the Deping Needle belonging to the Royal Society and found the North point to dep 26° below the Horizon, but the instrument cannot be used at sea to any great degree of accuracy on account of the motion of the Ship which hinders the Needle from resting;

however as the Ship was pretty steady and by means of a swinging table I had made for that purpose we could be certain of the dep to two degrees at most. The observed Latd and that by account nearly agrees.

Wednesday 26th. Winds SE to SSE. Course S 31° W. Distce in miles 77. Latd in 1°21' S. Longd in West from Greenwich 30°18'. Bearings at Noon Do N 25°30' E Dt 385 leagues.

First part light airs and clowdy weather, the remainder a Moderate breeze and clowdy. After we had got an Observation and it was no longer doubted that we were to the southward of the Line, the Ceremony on this occasion practised by all Nations was not omitted: every one that could not prove upon a Sea Chart that he had before crossed the Line, was either to pay a bottle of Rum or be ducked in the sea, which former case was the fate of by far the greatest part on board, and as several of the Men choose to be ducked and the weather was favourable for that purpose, this ceremony was performed on about 20 to 30 to the no small deversion of the rest.

SYDNEY PARKINSON: *JOURNAL OF A VOYAGE TO THE SOUTH SEAS*

On the 21st [October], we reached the S.E. trade wind, and continued our course without any remarkable occurrence till the 8th of November; then we discovered land at about eight leagues distance, and spoke with the crew of a Portugueze fishing vessel, of whom Mr. Banks bought a great quantity of fish, among which were dolphins and breams, which afforded much speculation to our naturalists.[1]

JOSEPH BANKS: *THE ENDEAVOUR JOURNAL 1768–1771*[2]

25. This morn about 8 O'Clock crossed the Æquinoctial line in about 33 degrees West Longitude from Greenwich, at the rate of four knotts which our seamen said was an uncommonly good breeze, the Thermometer standing at 29 . . .

This Evening the ceremony of ducking the ship's company was performed as always customary on

[1] So Sydney Parkinson does not describe crossing the equator at all.

[2] This is all terrific stuff.

crossing the line, when those who have crossd it before Claim a right of ducking all that have not, the whole of the ceremony I shall describe.

About dinner time a list was brought into the cabbin containing the names of every body and thing aboard the ship, in which the dogs and catts were not forgot; to this was affixd a petition, sign'd 'the ships company,' desiring leave to examine every body in that List that it might be known whether or not they had crossd the line before. This was immediately granted; every body was then calld upon the quarter deck and examind by one of the lieutenants who had crossd, he markd every name either to be duckd or let off according as their qualifications directed. Captn Cooke and Doctor Solander were on the Black list, as were my self my servants and doggs, which I was oblig'd to compound for by giving the Duckers a certain quantity of Brandy for which they willingly excusd us the ceremony.

Many of the Men however chose to be duckd rather than give up 4 days' allowance of wine which was the price fixd upon, and as for the boys they were always duckd of course, so that about 21 underwent the ceremony which was performd thus:

A block was made fast to the end of the Main Yard and a long line reved through it, to which three Cross pieces of wood were fastned, one of which was put between the leggs of the man who was to be duckd and to this he was tyed very fast, another was for him to hold in his hands and the third was over his head least the rope should be hoisted too near the block and by that means the man be hurt. When he was fastned upon this machine the Boatswain gave the command by his whistle and the man was hoisted up as high as the cross piece over his head would allow, when another signal was made and immediately the rope was let go and his own weight carried him down, he was then immediately hoisted up again and three times served in this manner which was every man's allowance. Thus ended the diversion of the day, for the ducking lasted till almost night, and sufficiently diverting it certainly was to see the different faces that were made on this occasion, some grinning and exulting in their hardiness whilst others were almost suffocated and came up ready enough to have compounded after the first or second duck, had such proceeding been allowable.

JOHN HAWKESWORTH: *AN ACCOUNT OF THE VOYAGES UNDERTAKEN BY THE ORDER OF HIS PRESENT MAJESTY FOR MAKING DISCOVERIES IN THE SOUTHERN HEMISPHERE*

On the 25th, we crossed the line with the usual ceremonies[3] in longitude 29° 30', when, by the result of several good azimuths, the variation was 2° 24'.

THOMAS TIMKINS: *OBSERVATIONS OF A GENTLE ENLIGHTENMENT CAT ON BOARD THE ENDEAVOUR, PURELY FOR SCIENTIFIC PURPOSES, 1768–71*

I will never forgive those bastards for this. I will never forgive them, not as long as I live.[4]

[3] Oddly, Hawkesworth declines to tell us what happened here, despite the vivid details in his sources.

[4] Poor Timkins. Poor, poor Timkins.

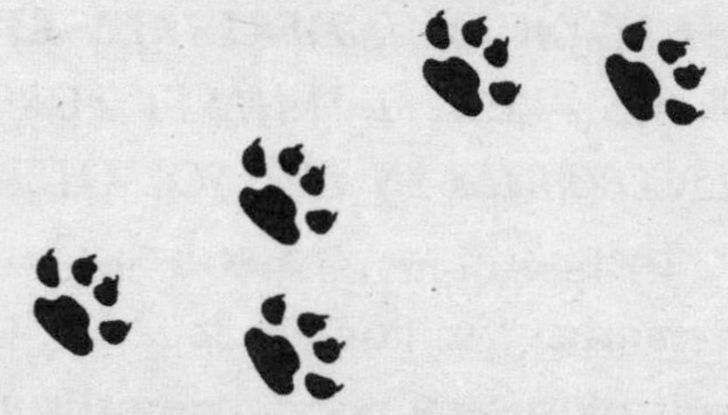

Chapter Three

I awoke to find Wiggy entering the room by the back door, which was all very odd. Especially looking at him sideways from a horizontal position on the floor. It was an unusual perspective, and it made the kitchen seem huge. It's funny how rarely one looks at one's own kitchen ceiling, isn't it? I could also see – under one of the base units – an old-fashioned wooden clothes peg, thick with dust and grease, that must have been there for years.

'Alec!' he said. 'I'm here. How are you? Thank goodness you're all right.'

I tried to lift my head, but it wouldn't co-operate. Instead, a pain shot through the left side of it – through my cheek and ear – which made me think (quite rationally), Well, I shan't try that again.

'Can you get up?' Wiggy asked urgently.

'No, I'll stay here,' I said, not moving. 'I'd prefer to stay here. There's a very interesting clothes peg over there that I'm keeping an eye on.'

'Oh, all right,' he said, confused. 'Are you sure? Shouldn't you sit up?'

I considered my reply for a moment or two. But, remembering the pain, I said, 'Yes, I'm sure. So tell me what happened.'

I closed my eyes while Wiggy told me what he had seen on the cameras. I was very keen to know whether he had seen the kitten poison my doggie, because if he *had* seen this (and not called me), I would be obliged to get up off the floor right then and kill him. But for the time being, I assumed he had not seen the poisoning – and in this, thank goodness, I was right. He had switched on the PCI equipment (Plan Cat Intruder) just in time to see the stewy old woman come in and start ransacking the place.

'So that's who hit me?' I said.

'Yes, the old woman!'

'How did she get in?'

'Back door?'

'Where's Tetty?'

'Gone.'

'Just like that?'

'Just like that!'

This was oddly upsetting. 'I think she used me,' I said.

'Of course she did.'

'I feel *used,* Wiggy.'

'Well, you would.'

I sighed, and tried to think of other things. Something other than how much I would miss my kitten's furry little tum and enormous eyes. 'They got the pamphlet!' I groaned.

'Why didn't you hide it better?' he said.

'I don't know.'

'What do you think they want it for?'

I tried moving again, while Wiggy had a look round the kitchen.

'This is even more untidy than it was before,' he remarked.

I let it pass. I had managed to drag myself to a sitting position, my back against the radiator. A new pain punched me in the face.

'What on earth did she hit me with?' I said.

Wiggy picked a volume off the table. 'Um, I think it was *The Endeavour Journal of Joseph Banks 1768–1771*, edited by J. C. Beaglehole, volume one.' He looked at it with surprise. 'Blimey, is Beaglehole a real name?'

'Show me,' I said.

He held it up.

'Oh no,' I said. 'That was from the London Library!'

I leapt up and grabbed the book from him to make sure it had suffered no damage – and I have to say, it's astonishing how one's librarianship instincts kick in at a time like this. Until that moment, I had hardly been able to move, but mention a library book in peril and I find considerable inner resources.

An hour later, Wiggy and I were having a cup of tea and sitting at the kitchen table. I was feeling OK – especially on discovering that the London Library would be requiring no awkward explanations. Wiggy had tidied up, which was jolly nice of him, but I was relieved that, when he swept the floor with a dustpan and brush, he didn't find the clothes peg. As we sat together, he was stacking the research stuff on the table again, reading out each title as he did so. Wiggy's habit of verbalising everything can be a bit annoying – 'Corn flakes HERE; porridge THERE' – but, as it meant that I could close my eyes and still know what was going on, I did not object. As he stacked the books, he intoned, 'Banks journal ONE, Banks journal TWO; journal of Sydney PARKINSON; book about COOK, another book about COOK; Hawkesworth's *Voyages* volume ONE; Hawkesworth TWO; Hawkesworth THREE; another book about COOK; something about LONDON LUNAR SOCIETY; book about JOHNSON; another book about JOHNSON; another book about JOHNSON; blimey, *another* book about JOHNSON—'

I stopped him. 'What's that about the Lunar Society?'

'Oh,' he said, and lifted several large tomes off the pile. 'Here we are.'

I had never seen it before. Closely printed on yellowed paper, it was the proceedings of the 'London Lunar Society', dating from the late 1760s. I frowned at it, and tried to focus on the question of where it could have come from. I did the classic thing of glancing at the ceiling, as if an eighteenth-century publication of rare historic interest could have landed in my kitchen from above. I had, of course, heard of the famous Lunar Society that met in Birmingham around this time – composed of great scientific minds, inventors, artisans and so on. The book by Jenny Uglow (*The Lunar Men*) was in one of the untidy piles in my study, and I'd been looking forward to reading it, my enthusiasm based not only on the self-evidently fascinating subject matter but also on the spectacular reviews. But I had never heard of a London branch of the Lunar Society. I certainly hadn't read this publication, nor had I borrowed it from any library; its presence in my kitchen was a mystery.

'Why was it a Lunar Society?' Wiggy asked. 'Were they all mad?'

'They met when the moon was full so that they could see better for getting home in the dark,' I said.

'Sounds a *bit* mad,' he said.

'Why?'

'Because they could have met indoors.'

I decided to leave it. 'Did the old woman bring this?' I said.

'Not that I saw.'

Wiggy finished the tidying and refilled the kettle. I was – and this surprised me – really grateful to him for being there.

'I saw her arrive, and have the argument with the kitten—'

'What argument?'

'—and then she went straight to the cereals cupboard and got the *Nine Lives* pamphlet.'

'So she knew where it was?'

'Yes. Tetty told her.'

'If she knew where it was, why all the mess?'

'She did all that afterwards.'

'Really?'

'Yeah.'

'So it wasn't because she was searching?'

'No, why?'

'Ugh.'

Wiggy didn't see why I found this annoying. 'Anyway, then she heard you coming in at the front door, so she put Tetty under her arm, and picked up this Beaglehole . . .' He broke off, tittering. 'Honestly, what a name!'

I didn't join in. The name of the scholarly Beaglehole had no comical dimension as far as I was concerned.

'Sorry. She picked up that book there and hid behind the kitchen door.'

He got up and demonstrated.

'So you come in *here,* and she's *here,* and I'm saying, on the phone, "She's behind you." And she steps forward—'

I interrupted. 'What you actually said was "Look out", Wiggy.'

'What?'

'You didn't say "She's behind you".'

Wiggy looked stricken. 'Didn't I?' he said.

I relented. I felt guilty. Somehow hurting Wiggy's feelings is unforgivable. 'Sorry,' I said. 'It's not important. Carry on.'

'So I say, "She's behind you," and she brings the book down on your poor head, Alec. And you just fall down!'

'I know I do. I mean, I know I did.'

'Thinking about it, you could have fallen against the edge of the table, Alec. It could have been a lot worse.'

He had a point there.

'Anyway, so then you're unconscious! But I needn't tell you about that because you know all about you being unconscious.'

'Well, yes and no.'

'But imagine what it was like for me! Watching all this! What should I do? Obviously, I wanted to come straight to you, but at the same time I wanted to see what else the horrible old woman would do next.'

'Why not record it?'

'That's what I decided to do, Alec, in the end. You're so clever! I set the computer to record the rest and dashed over. So I don't *think* she left this Lunar thing for you to find – or left it by mistake or something – but I can't be sure because when I left my place she'd just been kneeling in front of Tetty, with her head on the floor and her arms outstretched saying "All hail" and "Great Kitten Priestess of the Sacred Idol" and all that kind of thing.'

The kettle had boiled. He made tea. My head was still buzzing, but I was pretty sure I had just heard something that might qualify for the headline NEW INFORMATION ON DEMON KITTEN.

'She was *worshipping* Tetty?'

He plonked my cup down on the table.

'Oh, yes,' he said.

'Tetty, the tiny kitten, is' – and I repeated this carefully – 'a *priestess*, of a *sacred idol*?'

'Yep. Why not? High priestess, she said. Why?'

'Nothing. I just imagined somehow that Tetty was working for the old woman. Not the other way round.'

'No, it's definitely Tetty that's in charge.'

Wiggy opened my tin of biscuits, took a Rich Tea, and offered the tin to me. I shook my head.

'How do you know she's in charge?'

'Well, for a start, when the old woman arrived, Tetty really ticked her off! She said, "Mrs Fletcher, I am very, very disappointed in you." And the old woman said, "Oh, Kitty dear!" And Tetty growled, "Don't you Kitty me, Mrs F. The book's in with the porridge oats. Oh my giddy aunt, get a ruddy move on or you'll know the reason why."'

I took a deep breath and tried to control my patience. It seems to be my lot in life to deal with people who can *never* give information in the right order. Wiggy had discovered the woman's name, and it wasn't the first thing he'd told me! In fact, he probably still hadn't realised that the name 'Mrs Fletcher' was a useful thing to know. He had also learned the unusual nature of the relationship between the woman and the demon kitten – supplicant/slave to high priestess – but telling me this hadn't even been high up on his 'to do' list for the day. I wondered what other precious nuggets he was not bothering to impart.

'Did she happen to mention Bromley, Wiggy?'

He was so startled he choked on his biscuit. 'Yes! Sorry, I forgot that bit. She *did* mention Bromley, and I thought, Ooh, Alec will be interested in that, because he's always harping on about Bromley even though he didn't want to go there very much. Yes. The woman said, "I came all the way from Bromley *twice*, Kitty. I also jumped on that old man in that shop, just like you told me to." Sorry she called you an old man, Alec. And then Tetty said again not to call her Kitty, so that was when the old woman started calling her the "High Priestess to the Great Oh-Vera" instead.'

'"Vera"? There's a cult of *Vera*? Like Vera Lynn?'

'No. It was more like Oh-Vera. Great Oh-Vera.'

'And she actually knelt in front of her?'

'Oh yes. It was quite funny.'

'Can we go to your place and see what you recorded?'

'Of course, Alec. But what about your head?'

I said I was fine. But I made no move to get up from the kitchen table. My head was still swimming, and there was a sort of deadness to my left foot that was a bit peculiar. I clearly needed more time to recover. I looked at the Lunar Society proceedings, still under my hand, and felt a wave of anger. Why me? I mainly felt. More specifically, I thought, Why me *again*? Because (as I might have mentioned before) it did seem a bit unfair that this was happening. Why did evil talking cats keep involving me in their damned overcomplicated plots? A demonic kitten had invaded my home and stolen an invaluable piece of ETC apparatus relating to the subjugation of cats to Cat Masters; meanwhile I was constantly being nudged towards Bromley; and also towards the first voyage of Captain Cook, with no clue as to the connection between any of it! I mean, look at this damned thing. The London Lunar Society! What was I supposed to make of this? I scanned it impatiently: members' names included Signor Andreotti, Mr Hodge, Mr Timkins, Mrs Stella, Mr Nolly, and so on, and so on. (Mrs Stella was in smaller type.)

> President's name and editor of proceedings, Dr Hawkesworth. Published from St John's

> Gate, Clerkenwell, home of *The Gentleman's Magazine*, and edited by Dr Hawkesworth, the acclaimed essayist, that great literary ornament of the Age, universally known as *The Adventurer*.

As I held this ancient document in my hand, I knew I was lost. I felt almost dizzy. A connection! A connection at last! The eighteenth-century Cat Master who succeeded Henry Fielding in 1754 – and whose identity I had, so far, hopelessly failed to ascertain – was none other than Dr John Hawkesworth, author of *An Account of the Voyages Undertaken By the Order of His Present Majesty for Making Discoveries in the Southern Hemisphere*!

Wiggy got up and went into the living room, where (as I later discovered) he did some discreet tidying up, and switched on the TV for the news. I was pleased to be left alone. My mind raced. Hawkesworth – I must look him up! All I could remember, for the present, was a bit of a story: that Hawkesworth finished writing up the *Voyages*, and was paid an absolute mint for doing the job, but then – after publication – he just died. There was some sort of hoo-ha about the *Voyages*, wasn't there? Yes, there was. A definite hoo-ha.

The London literary hack who had the job of turning the journals into popular literature was so savagely attacked in the press that it killed him. And didn't Cook disown what he'd written, as well? And didn't Johnson drop him, having been his friend? I grabbed the copy of Boswell on the table and looked up Hawkesworth in the index. It said:

> **Hawkesworth, Dr. J.** (1715?–73): ***Adventurer***, 166, 178; **Bromley**, 171; **Cook's voyages**, 537, 722; **Courtenay**, 159; **Ivy Lane Club**, 137; **S.J. [Samuel Johnson]**, 159, 166, 172, 437, 572; **Swift**, 595; ***Universal Visiter***, 129

I suppose it was too much to ask that, alphabetically between 'Bromley' and 'Cook's voyages', it should have listed 'Cat Master', but in my present state of epiphany, I half expected it to be there.

I held the London Lunar Society paper before my eyes. I didn't call to Wiggy. I wasn't ready to share anything with him yet; I wanted to have this moment to myself. Afterwards, I was glad I did. Here was a scientific society, in London, convened by an eminent man of letters, and the members were all, quite clearly, cats. Clever, clever cats. Subjects for future papers included:

a proposed solution to the Longitude Problem (Mr Timkins);

thoughts on thigmotaxis [thigmotaxis!], *being the motion or orientation of an organism in response to a touch stimulus* (Mr Cuddles);

a modest proposal for the uses of steam in the extermination of the flea (Mr Scratchy);

chemical composition of the fur ball (Mr MacJockie);

the ability of a single cat to reduce a Chippendale armoire to matchwood with just twenty well-aimed blows (Mr Bruise);

the late collapse of a house in Leadenhall caused by concerted purring of 24 cats, with diagrams (Mr Hodge);

why cats' eyes reflect light (Dr Hawkesworth); and:

the true place of yowling in the spectrum of agreeable vocal musical production (Sr Andreotti);

and finally, in smaller type:

a female's recollections of sitting upon the lap of Mr Benjamin Franklin; also demonstration with a Leyden Jar, if time (Mrs Stella).

I sighed. My head was throbbing. I gave my deadened left leg a shake to get the circulation going. Here was a lot to take in, suddenly.

'Is that thing interesting?' Wiggy asked, putting his head round the door.

I felt like crying. It had been an emotional day, what with Watson being poisoned, and my kitchen being trashed, and my head being coshed, but what really upset me was that this bloody document was not just 'interesting', it was *unbelievably interesting.*

'It's very, very interesting,' I said, sniffing. I put my hand up to my face. I realised it was shaking.

'Alec!' he said, coming over to sit beside me. 'Watson will be OK. And I'll tell you what: *Miss Marple*'s on in a minute. It's the one with the body in the library, but I can't remember what it's called.'

I wasn't sure if he was joking.

'*The Body in the Library*?' I said.

'Yes, that's right,' he agreed. 'Can you remember what it's called?'

I tried to pull myself together. Giving Wiggy the lowdown on these new discoveries was going to take patience and a lot of mental strength.

'I'm all right,' I said, but I found I was still crying. In fact, I was crying and laughing at the same time – something I had seen done in films, but never in real life.

Wiggy touched my arm. Tears trickled down my cheeks.

'So are we still at square one?' he said brightly. 'Or was this thing quite interesting?'

I gave up trying to hold it in. 'Oh Wiggy,' I wailed. 'Wiggy!'

He looked at me with alarm.

'Wiggy, I've never read anything more interesting in my life!'

We watched the news together, and of course there was an item about Bromley. A house had fallen down in the middle of the night, and experts were baffled. No one had perished in the collapse, as the elderly spinster who lived there had been absent at the time, but neighbours were in shock. The mystery was that there was no explosion; it was as if the house had suffered its own private earthquake and had been shaken to the ground.

I turned to Wiggy. I gave him a meaningful look.

'I know!' he said. 'Bromley *again*.'

There had been no witnesses to the collapse; neighbours could only remember (unhelpfully) a loud, low, rumbling, humming sound in the middle of the night – 'Like the sound of bees,' they said. 'But lower.' Engineers insisted that only an explosion could have brought a solid old house down, but others claimed that they hadn't heard one. At the end of the item was a shot of a rescue worker in the ruins, pausing in his digging to stroke the head of a thin yellow cat that was watching his progress from a wall.

'Wiggy,' I said. 'I think it's time we went to Bromley.'

'All right,' he said. 'Isn't it terrible that a house can just fall down, though?'

'I don't think it did just fall down. I think the humming noise people heard was – well, I think it was cats.' And I showed him the Lunar Society list of papers, indicating the relevant item concerning the catastrophic effect of mass concerted harmonic purring on the vertical integrity of brick-built structures.

'This Lunar Society,' I explained, 'was not quite like other learned societies of the period. It was run by a Cat Master, and it's my opinion, from looking at this, that all the members were cats.'

'Evil talking cats?'

'Well, very clever cats, definitely. Look here. One of them even has a solution to the longitude problem.'

'Blimey.'

'The Cat Master's name was, look, John Hawkesworth. It's all falling into place, Wiggy! Look! There's even a paper on *thigmotaxis!*'

'I thought that was a person.'

'So did I. But the important thing is this Hawkesworth. He was the man who wrote up the voyages of Captain Cook, he came to a mysterious sticky end, and he had connections with Bromley that I haven't yet looked into, but I should.' At this, a thought struck me. 'Hang on,' I said.

I left Wiggy looking at the list while I hobbled on my weird dead leg into the study to use the computer. Hadn't I downloaded information about Bromley churchyard? The churchyard that had suffered 'abominations'? It took a while to retrieve it, and I was a bit distracted by Wiggy chuckling over the idea of a lecture on the chemistry of furballs, but eventually, there it was. I scanned it and found the name at once. There was a monument to John Hawkesworth at the church of St Peter and St Paul in Bromley.

He had been buried in the churchyard, but his grave had been bombed during the Second World War. But there was still a monument to him inside the church:

To the memory of John Hawksworth, LL.D. who died the 17th of November 1773, aged 58 years. That he lived useful and ornamental to society, in an eminent degree, was among the boasted felicities of the present age; that he laboured for the benefit of posterity, let his own pathetic admonition at once record and realise.

From *The Adventurer, No. 140.*
The hour approaches, in which, whatever praise or censure I have acquired by these compositions, if they are remembered at all, will be remembered with equal indifference, and the tenour of them only will afford me comfort. Time, who is impatient to date my last paper, will shortly moulder the hand that is now writing it in the dust, and still the breast that now throbs at the reflection: but let not this be read as something that relates to another; for a few years only can divide the eye that is now reading from the hand that has written. This

awful truth, however obvious and however reiterated, is yet frequently forgotten; for, surely, if we did not lose our remembrance, or at least our sensibility, that view should always predominate in our lives, which alone can afford us comfort when we die.

Bromley in Kent, Mar. 8, 1754.

Also buried in the churchyard, I noticed, was Dr Johnson's wife Elizabeth (Tetty) – after whom I had innocently named a visiting evil kitten who was in reality (apparently) priestess of a cult. Was this a coincidence? Was I operating under some sort of influence when I named her thus? Had I been predestined to quit my own pleasant and brightly lit modern existence and follow this line of enquiry into the scary, dark, long-ago alleyways of eighteenth-century literary London, where cats with an interest in longitude went on scientific expeditions to the South Seas, and houses could be made to fall down by fiendish organised purring?

'Anything?' asked Wiggy when I returned to the living room.

'Hawkesworth is definitely our man,' I said. 'He's buried in the churchyard.'

'Well done,' said Wiggy. 'You're very good at this, you know, Alec. Piecing things together.'

'Yes, but what do the cats want? Why are they digging? Who brought me the evidence of the Lunar Society? What is the cult of the sacred idol? Who is Oh-Vera? Why did cats bring that house down today? If thigmotaxis is a scientific *thing* in animals, who is my mystery employer Mr Thigmo Taxis? Why does Tetty sound like a cockney fifties villainess? And finally, what on earth can be learned from the chemical composition of a furball?'

It was then that Wiggy said a very sensible thing. 'I think, when we go to Bromley, we shouldn't take Watson. Let him recover at the vet's. He's too vulnerable if we take him with us.'

I agreed. Part of me couldn't help being amused at the idea of Bromley as a supernatural danger zone, but Wiggy was right, nevertheless. Watson had been poisoned already; there was no dishonour in his discharge. I would miss his company, but it would give me peace of mind to know that he was safe. Leaving him at the vet's *over Christmas*, however, would be so ruinously expensive that I might have to sell the car afterwards to pay for it.

* * *

I filled a box with books, called the vet's to ask them to keep Watson there for the next few days, and we made our way to Wiggy's flat. The plan was to watch the recording he had made, then sleep for a few hours and set off for Bromley as early as possible in the morning.

As we set off, Wiggy said, 'So, this Hawksmith—'

'Hawkesworth.'

'Sorry, Hawkesworth. What's the big mystery about his death?'

Sometimes when I'm driving I don't really like to talk. But I've found that the act of concentrating on the road can also make me think more clearly – it helps me focus and remember – and that was definitely the case that day. Fragments of things I had read were drawn up from my subconscious.

'Right, well. I don't know much, but as I recall, he was paid an enormous sum for writing the *Voyages*.'

'Like how much?'

'Well, remember, this was in the 1770s.'

'Yes.'

'Oh, I don't know, but it was huge. Thousands.'

'Thousands of pounds?'

'Yes. I think it was six thousand.'

'Wow.'

'I know. And then he wrote the books and they were published and immediately he was attacked from all sides, really pounded into the ground. Some people criticised them for being too lewd, because of all the goings-on in Tahiti, and then—'

'What goings-on do you mean?'

'Oh.' I had sort of assumed that Wiggy knew about the first voyage. He had, after all, written that bit of screenplay that you might remember I decided not to include in this narrative earlier on, for fear of holding things up.

'Well, Tahiti was the destination of the first voyage. They were sent to Tahiti to do an astronomical observation. Afterwards, Cook did a map of the whole of New Zealand, and then he mapped the east coast of Australia, but the main thing was to set up an observatory in Tahiti and watch the transit of Venus.'

'Alec, have you always known about this?'

I had to think. It was a good question. I was talking as if all this transit-of-Venus stuff were common knowledge, but a month before I probably hadn't known any of it.

'No,' I said. 'I've just done a lot of reading lately. Anyway, so they're in Tahiti and the natives are, to put it mildly, incredibly friendly, especially the women. The myth that comes down is that the only payment the women wanted for sex was iron nails from the ship, and the result was that the ship nearly fell apart.'

Wiggy laughed.

'But it wasn't all friendly. The hardest thing for Cook and Banks and the others was that the natives kept stealing stuff, like optical instruments and guns and so on. They didn't seem to have an understanding of right and wrong.'

'So what did Hawksmoor do wrong?' asked Wiggy.

'Who?'

'Hawksmoor.'

'Wiggy, it's Hawkesworth!'

'Right. Sorry. What did Hawkesworth do wrong?'

'Oh, I think people said it was a dirty book, basically. And Cook himself didn't like what he'd done, and people said there were "howlers" in it. I can't remember what else he was accused of. But it broke his heart, I suppose. He died within the year. And then, from being quite the literary big cheese, he got buried in bloody *Bromley* and fell into complete obscurity, utter nothingness, which has lasted ever since. There's almost nothing written about him.'

'From hero to zero?' Wiggy asked.

It wasn't an expression I'd heard before, and I can't say I liked it, but I was so glad Wiggy was following me that I happily agreed. 'Yes, from hero to zero,' I said.

We were nearing Wiggy's flat now. He guided me to a parking space behind a row of shops. His flat was upstairs from a photocopying emporium. We parked and got out of the car.

'Aren't Cat Masters in league with the Devil?' Wiggy said as we lugged the box of books out of the boot. 'You'd think, with connections like that, Hawksmith could have saved himself.'

'Hawkesworth,' I said again as I slammed the boot door down. 'But that's a good point, Wiggy. That's a very, very, *very* good point.'

Upstairs we watched the recording Wiggy had made. In fact, we watched it three times, and after Wiggy had retired to bed I watched it again for a fourth. It was horrible – but fascinating – to see oneself unconscious. It was fascinating – but horrible – to learn more about what was really going on. My previous impression of Mrs Fletcher had been of motiveless malignity; now I could see she was a mere pawn in a larger game. She deferred to Tetty; she was scared of her. She stammered when she spoke to her. As the recording began, Mrs Fletcher was cowering in the middle of the room, the book still in her hand, after delivering the blow to my head. Tetty was on the draining board, beside the *Nine Lives* pamphlet. Mrs Fletcher's handbag was on a chair. The place was in the total disarray that I had seen when I'd come in. But on the table, among the disordered books, there was no obvious sign of the Lunar Society proceedings.

'He ain't dead, is he?' Tetty rasped.

Mrs Fletcher put down the book and searched for a hanky up her sleeve. Nervously she wiped her nose. And then she bent down to take a look at me.

'Oh Kitty!' she said. 'I don't know! I'm not sure! There's no blood or anything. He seems to be breathing. Have you got a mirror?'

'Oh, for crying out loud,' said Tetty, and jumped down to the floor. 'Do I look like I've got a bleeding mirror? Let's get out of this dump.'

The angle and position of the camera were not helpful here, because the body on the floor (me) was almost out of sight, but each time I watched the tape I pitifully hoped that when Tetty said the word 'dump', my prone body on the kitchen floor would register this hurtful insult. Of course, it never did.

Mrs Fletcher was still dithering.

'Shouldn't we call for an ambulance or something? Kitty, I hit him on the head!'

'Look, we needed to get the pamphlet. That's the only reason I come here. And we've ruddy got it, so let's go. It's the full moon on Wednesday! This is IT!'

'You're sure this bloke won't put two and two together?'

It gives me no pleasure to report how Tetty replied to this. She screeched with laughter. 'This bloke?' she said.

She walked right over to me and looked into my face.

'This bloke?' she repeated.

And then she raised her top lip, to bare her little teeth, and hissed at me.

It was easy to focus on Tetty during this scene, which was why I asked Wiggy to rewind it, so that we could watch Mrs Fletcher instead. Would she produce the Lunar Society thing? No. But she did do something interesting. She started to shake with fear, and also to move her lips – as if silently repeating words to herself.

Tetty, beside me on the floor, was pacing up and down, regarding me with contempt. And then she seemed to reach a decision.

'Mrs Fletcher, produce the Oh-Vera.'

The old lady's face crumpled. She was in serious distress. Watching such a strong reaction, I have to say I was in pretty serious distress as well, and I didn't even know what they were talking about.

'Oh, please don't, Kitty. Please don't. You got it for him, and he's coming soon. We're not supposed to!'

'Oh, cheese it, you witch,' said Tetty. 'And do what you're bleeding well told.'

Mrs Fletcher reached into her bag and produced an object, around nine inches long, wrapped in a piece of printed cloth.

'But Kitty!' she said.

'*Ma-MOO!*' said Tetty.

This strange word had an electrifying effect. Not only on Mrs Fletcher, but on the two of us watching it, too. I was very glad Watson hadn't heard it; he'd have barked the place down. Tetty seemed to swell in size when she said it.

And then, as a figurine was unwrapped by Mrs Fletcher, Tetty began to sing a song: '*Taowdee waow, tettata waow, t'eva heinéa waow!*'

Wiggy and I were both horrified. Wiggy kept saying, 'Alec! Alec, wake up! You've got to wake up!'

I didn't wake up.

'*Te tanè a waow, teina ye waow, e tottee era waow!*' Tetty continued.

There on the kitchen floor, I was unaware that a ritual was being performed on me, in my own house, by the tiny little kitten I had cuddled; the tiny little kitten I had taken under my own roof out of sheer compassion on a frosty night.

'Leave it there, please, Kitty!' Mrs Fletcher said. 'I think there's someone outside.'

Tetty stopped singing and listened.

'You're right,' she said. 'There's someone there.'

As she paused in the proceedings, there was just one last chance for Alec (me) to regain consciousness and grab the kitten by its tiny throat. But it will not surprise you to hear that Alec (I) remained prone and lifeless on the floor. And that when Tetty, standing alongside my feet, flexed her front claws, took steady aim and, chanting '*Ooàteea te tirre no'è*', drove a claw directly into my left ankle joint, I still didn't move, although Mrs Fletcher let out a terrible groan. In her hands the figurine twitched but she held it tight.

In a blur they were gone. I (the viewer) rubbed my ankle.

'They've gone,' said Wiggy. 'Oh Alec. I had no idea.'

'Well, obviously nor did I!' I said. On the screen, there was no movement. Just me, on the floor.

'Look, how long did it take you to arrive at my house? Do you think the sound they heard outside was you arriving?'

'It might have been. I'm not sure. I need to think. But I think it took about fifteen minutes to get to you because I just missed a bus and had to wait for the next one. Oh Alec. Isn't it dreadful just watching you there like this? I don't really want to see myself coming in the door. Can we switch it off when I come in? It's too *weird*. What was all that chanting?'

I'm afraid to say, there was a small part of this that I felt I needed to return to.

'Wiggy,' I said. 'You came by *bus*?'

'It's sometimes the quickest way, Alec. It's very hard to park near your house, you know that.'

'You saw me attacked with a book and you—'

'Alec.' Wiggy was still looking at the screen.

'Wiggy, look at me,' I said. 'I could have been killed!'

'Alec, look. Stop and look.'

And so I looked at the screen again, and I jumped in the air. Because there, in my kitchen, walking on strong, silent paws, was a large and beautiful tabby-and-white cat, its tail up, its face tilted, its supreme intelligence translated into every movement of its body.

'Oh my God,' I said.

It was a cat whose classic tabby markings I would know anywhere; a cat I had thought never to see again.

'Roger!' I gasped.

I am still emotional when I remember this first moment of seeing him. Roger had survived the death plunge, after all. He was here. He had nudged my back door open, carrying the Lunar Society document in his teeth. On seeing me on the floor, he dropped it and trotted to my side.

'Alec,' he said. (*Roger remembered me!*)

'I'm so sorry,' he said. (*Roger was sorry!*)

He set a caring paw on my forehead. (*Roger loved me!*)

He sniffed me carefully, and then he said, 'Oh no!' (*This was worrying.*)

He sniffed along my body until he reached my ankle and then let out a cry. 'Not the Oviri!' (*This was even more worrying.*)

He picked up the Lunar Society thing and jumped on to the table with it. He then peered around the room until he located the camera, and he looked straight into it.

We both sat back in our seats.

'If anyone is watching this,' he said, 'Alec is in terrible peril. Doctors cannot help. There is good news and bad news. The bad news is that the Cat Master known as the Adventurer is the cause of all this. The good news is that, after this *outrage*' – he pointed at me, on the floor – 'I can no longer sit quietly in the shadows, pretending to be somebody called Thigmo Taxis.'

He looked down at me on the floor and said, conversationally, 'I'm sorry about all those "nows" in my emails, by the way, Alec. I was using voice-recognition software, and every time

I miaowed, it wrote "now". It was incredibly annoying.'

He jumped down again and nudged my nose with his own. Watching it, I touched my nose with my fingers. How could I not have known?

'I will save you, Alec.'

He left the room. Thirty seconds later the figure of Wiggy arrived on screen, and he insisted we switch it off. So we did. And for quite a while, we sat in stunned silence.

'Are we going to have a look at your leg?' Wiggy said at last.

I said that I supposed we must. All I could say was that it felt a bit numb.

'It might not be anything,' Wiggy said.

'Right,' I agreed.

Then I took off my shoe and sock, and rolled up my trouser-leg and we both screamed.

My whole foot and ankle had turned a bright, vivid yellow, and where Tetty had stabbed me there was a hole. And around the hole was a small, wet, bright red, circular protuberance that looked like – well, I'm afraid to say, it looked very like a *mouth.*

Part Two

Documents

Document One

The Circumnavigation Journal of Mr Thomas Timkins, late of the London Lunar Society

(with the irregular spelling and 'ſs and 's's sorted out, for *eaſe of reeding*)

April 7th, 1768

Lively night at Lunar Society indeed. The wig of Mr Tinkle descending to the floor, quite in the middle of his practical demonstration of the bleaching properties of feline micturition, brought much merriment to our proceedings. 'He has pissed on his own wig!' called some. For myself, I kept silent, as so did the good Doctor H., who feeling pity for the confused lecturer stepped in and restoring the dripping and stinking wig to poor T's pate made a solemn disquisition upon the nature of good fellowship which quite shamed them who had laughed, and several slunk into the shadows, their heavy tails quite dragging in the dust. The accident of the pissed wig was, however, so very comical that after all others had departed, the good doctor and I laughed about it in private for quite an hour by the clock. In the end, the doctor threatening to become hysterical with his memories of the unfortunate speaker, I had to swipe him sharply with my paw to restore his mood to soberness, for which he thanked me humbly, and did forgive the blood.

April 25th, 1768

I am to sail on the *Endeavour*! And I am but two years old! Dr H. has shown me on a map where I will sail. 'You see all this wide oceanic portion with nothing marked upon it?' he says. 'That's where you shall be, young Timkins! That's where you shall be! A small black cat on a small wooden ship with an emotionally unpredictable captain and a gent collecting plants!' When the case is put in this wise to me, my ears go flat and my back legs begin to agitate. It is to be a great scientific expedition, however, and the doctor says that were it not for certain weighty literary expectations laid on him here in London, he would without hesitation enlist on board himself. 'It will be a great adventure!' he pronounces if ever I advance some small misgiving concerning the safety of the enterprise, or ask what consequence my own attendance within it can achievably produce. 'These are the days of miracle!' he cries. 'Moreover, Timkins, forget not that the solver of the Longitude Problem receives a prize of Twenty Thousand Pounds!'

I fear I am to blame for this enthusiasm in Dr H. For, on joining the Society, I had no great subject on which to speak to the learned group and finding that many were desirous of inquiring narrowly into mere material aspects of our own species – potential destructive power of purring, scientific properties of cat urine, ability of cats to land on their feet when deliberately dropped from high walls upside down – I felt our little bark of knowledge might capsize at once were not some braver soul to lean out wide to catch a countering breeze. And thus I found myself proposing a solution to the Longitude Problem! Dr H. was overjoyed at my ambition and offered all assistance. A corner of his home in Bromley became my own, in which to work for six whole months, and never had I seen such a great house before. In case there should be any doubt in its being a great house, it is even named 'The Grete House'! I was supplied with astronomical charts and a costly telescope. I was brought intelligence of every quackish solution already considered by the Board of Longitude, including large complicated golden clocks and funny rocking chairs on gimbals for viewing the heavens while at sea. None of these solutions disturbed, however, my own revolutionary theory of how to stop His Majesty's ships from running aground, a theory which I propounded at the last full moon at first to a confused and worried silence and then to great applause, congratulation and huzzahs.

My solution to the Longitude Problem was indeed revolutionary: it was to acknowledge that there was no problem. In my view no sailor requires the means to calculate by long-winded celestial observation or by unreliable timepieces his ship's precise position, in degrees and minutes, west or east of an invented meridian! All a ship needs is a cat, because:

i. cats always know precisely where they are,
ii. cats never knock into things,
iii. cats hate getting wet.

As I set out my hypothesis, I was aware that all held their breath, although not entirely on account of my brilliance; it was partly on account of the stink of Mr Tinkle's wig, which ought by rights no longer to be worn in confined quarters where the air is common to more than two or three there gathered. And so I continued from hypothesis to proof by way of experiment, in which experiment I must confess I had sufficient confidence that I had already – departing from accepted empirical practice – written up the astonishing results for distribution at the conclusion of the evening.

I turned to my audience. All members here present, I said, had entered the room by means of the usual corridor, with which they were familiar. They shrugged and agreed that they knew this corridor well. But I had more to ask. 'You could navigate it blindfold?' I inquired. Again, with shrugs, they assented. But what if it had been re-arranged, I said. As it happened, once we had been shut into our meeting room on this particular evening I had instructed the keeper of the inn to disorder all the chests and chairs along this corridor; to roll up the rugs; place precious antique vases along its length. I then set a blindfold upon Mr Tinkle (and in removing his wig made it possible for Dr H. to take it between thumb and finger and discreetly drop it from a window). I then asked Mr T. to walk back along the corridor to the top of the stairs, while we others watched him, some of us with a paw to our mouths in amazement for his performance was so beautiful to behold. Mr T. was bold and yet he was cautious. What one observed in him was an innate navigational genius, as he deftly avoided all collisions, with large and small obstacles alike. The landlord had at one point created a veritable barricade, and Mr T. in his blinded state approached it gingerly, held his head first to this side and then to that, as if to learn everything about it; then he twisted himself to squeeze through the only gap, and all as I said completely without recourse to ocular confirmation!

But this was not the final experiment. I had ordered for a rowing boat to be readied at the Temple Stairs, and Dr H. took the oars while the rest of us sat facing forward. Again I blindfolded one of our party, in this case the splendid Mr Hodge, and gave him full command of the vessel. I acknowledge that the incredible danger in which I placed my fellows on this occasion was intended to heighten their appreciation of the results, which were indeed remarkable. From the moment Dr H. began to ply the water and propel us across its darkened surface, Mr Hodge could guide him safely, with such confidence that it struck all of us with pride. Those of us whose eyes were uncovered were sometimes dazzled by the moonlight on the water, but Mr Hodge faltered not at all, guiding the doctor between ferries and larger boats, ever into safer channels. I was extremely pleased with the experiment. I grant that cat urine has interesting bleaching properties; that cats are inexplicably self-righting during an earthward plummet; that the musculature of the feline ear is a miracle of divine invention. But I believe I have proved that as instinctive navigators in an age of exploration we clever talking cats may well have found our true vocation on this earth.

July 21st, 1768

I am on board. I wonder if I've got on a bit early. It being Dr H.'s wish that I travel in the early stages anonymous on this ship, I climbed aboard here under cover of darkness at Deptford and I write this from the lower deck of the *Endeavour*, at the foot of a feature named the 'fore-hatch ladderway'.

I have rarely been so anxious in my life. I find that I have quite lost control of my own tail, which swishes of its own accord in a manner most distressing. I chose this spot (beneath the fore-hatch ladderway) because it provides shelter from the elements yet has easy potential for escape in the event of a capsize; it moreover provides an excellent vantage point for observing the busy life on board; it is also quite proximate to an oven. It all smells very new, as I suppose it should, this lower deck having been built specially for the voyage. As Dr H. has so often remarked in his splendid *Adventurer* essays, it is a very remarkable age that we live in, that can fit out a rough, square, collier boat and send it on learned expeditions towards uncharted waters!

I had imagined that Dr H. would secure me passage on the ship alongside the other men of science, but I discover they are not yet aboard and will join us at Plymouth and that in any case I am to play the part of humble ship's cat until I consider it safe to announce my genius to the good Captain, at which point I shall in all probability relieve him of the larger part of his duties, to his great contentment. I must therefore bide my time and, if I may allow myself an expression derived from the ballistic sciences, keep my powder dry.

Dr H., being very excited about our South Seas destination, presented me with sealed instructions of some small experiments he wishes me to perform on our arrival. How to conceal these instructions has been my first concern, having no quarters of my own, and the fore-hatch ladderway being no place to secrete such an important missive. In the end, I crept into the Great Cabin in the stern, where the Captain and his 'supernumerary' guests will abide, and finding a small cupboard open, I crept inside and deposited the document (addressed to myself, 'Thomas Timkins, Esq., FLLS[5]') just inside but out of sight, and now I must pray that no one else will find it.

[5] Fellow of the London Lunar Society.

I brought little aboard besides these plentiful writing materials, without which, of course, I could not write this journal. If my reader should be wondering how a cat can keep a journal, by the bye, and is asking himself how in practice it can be managed, I cannot oblige for I am subject to an unbreakable oath of secrecy upon this matter. All I can say is: no man ever saw a cat writing, and no man ever will! What I principally regret is bringing no reading matter aboard with me. There will be many days at sea when I will devoutly wish for the works of dear Dr H. for both stimulation and edification. By good fortune I do recollect some of his finer essays, having learned them by heart, but to have his immortal work beside me would be akin to having his real company for this journey of some weeks away from home. On reflection, the one thing I neglected to inquire of Dr H. was the proposed length of this journey, for this being July, I would sincerely hope to be home again by September, when it is my birthday.

July 25th, 1768

We have not yet left Deptford. Yesterday for the first time I saw the ship's master, James Cook, at close quarters, as he climbed the ladderway, having inspected the hold below. He spotted me and I went forward with my paw extended in order to shake his hand, and he said (I shall never forget his exact words, and I herewith record them for posterity), 'Whose fucking cat is this?' I must confess I was covered in confusion, and I am greatly ashamed to admit that in the face of such outright and shocking bad manners I bared my teeth at him and hissed. By great good fortune the ship's surgeon, Mr Monkhouse, happened to be passing from his surgeon's cabin and when he heard the great navigator addressing me thus, he came forward and, picking me up, said with great acuity and human kindness, 'The cat be mine, sir,' and by this a most unpleasant outcome was thankfully forestalled, as I fear I might otherwise have been angrily tossed overboard, so strong did the Captain's feelings seem to be when in the presence of a decorous and gentle feline. I was grateful to Mr Monkhouse for his ingenious intervention but, having said this, I must make note here that Mr Monkhouse being a Cumbrian by birth, and having been much at sea, he is not at all the sort of person I wish to associate with from among this company. He has a brother on board who is a mere midshipman! My intention of befriending Mr Banks and Dr Solander and the other learned 'supernumeraries' of the voyage may surely be much damaged were I to assort myself so early with the likes of mere Monkhouses from Cumbria.

I perceive there is much coarseness in seafaring fellows; they require the civilising influence of a cat bred to the highest Enlightenment values. When the Captain was gone, Mr Monkhouse took me to his surgeon's cabin and placed me on a rough operating table already stained with blood, saying, 'What be your name, then, young puss?' Looking back on the incident, I now strongly suspect Mr Monkhouse intended for this inquiry to be taken as an interrogative of the rhetorical variety, but I'm afraid I was raised a gentleman, so I merely replied, 'Thomas Timkins, sir, at your service,' and, his grip loosening from the surprise, I leapt off the table and escaped to the hold, where I hid among some barrels until dark.

As I write this now I am uncertain whether to persevere with this journey, but when I consider the shame of returning to London without testing my great navigational theory I find I must hold fast.

Already I have made some charts which I believe will be of incalculable value to the Admiralty upon the ship's return.

A bit of mackerel for tea, found discarded outside the gunners' cabin. Delicious.

July 29th, 1768

Having neglected my journal for a few days, I must report that we have gone nowhere. This is frustrating and again I am surprised at Dr H. for not enlisting me among the party who are due to board at Plymouth. Mr Cook, the famous First Lieutenant whom we call Captain, is now aboard, but I have not seen him since the day he called me a 'fucking cat', an insult that burns deeper with the passage of time instead of ameliorating. Mr Monkhouse has been looking for me, calling, 'Puss, puss, Thomas Timkins, where be you, Thomas Timkins?' but I have been too clever for him.

August 2nd, 1768

We are at sea but we keep stopping. Oh my GOD but the motion is horrible. And the SMELL. I have no idea what's going on. Rain thunders on the deck above, so what with the noise of the feet of the men as they run back and forth, and the creak of the wood and the general SHOUTING, and the infernal BELLS, it is enough to drive a sensible being totally distracted. I have no idea where we are except that someone mentioned Deal in my hearing, which is ridiculous if true, if it has taken a WEEK to get to DEAL, for I happen to know it takes just three hours by carriage to Deal from Dr H.'s house! How can anyone THINK on board a ship? I have tried to close my eyes and draw forth the inward map of my surroundings – England HERE, France over THERE – but not only do we swing round in the water, so that England is now THERE and France is HERE, but the action of closing my eyes has such a churning effect upon my guts that I am forever obliged to reopen them immediately.

Oh my GOD. Oh my GOD. Sailors dash about pulling ropes and shouting to one another; great wet sails are hoisted and lowered. The pitching as the ship sails forward is intolerable, but when we stop and drop anchor it's far worse because we rock from side to side and you can feel a great swell which makes the ship rise and fall, and I honestly think that rather than investigate Longitude, the great minds of our age should be busily inventing a way of getting around the world that does not involve putting a vessel made out of floating WOOD on to the surface of deep and unpredictable WATER, especially when the WIND for the sails is forever blowing unhelpfully from diverse directions. I spoke a few words with the surgeon today, which I know I had vowed not to do but he was patting me on the head in a kindly way at the time, and also mopping up the vomit I had inadvertently deposited on the deck.

August 26th, 1768, Plymouth

Mr Banks is aboard the ship at last but there is terrible news. Among his party are gentlemen, servants and artists, but also DOGS. I am thoroughly disheartened. Who on earth would take a dog on a ship? Having heard such good reports of the young Mr Banks, I have to declare that I was expecting much more from him than this. There are chickens on this ship. There is a goat. This is no place for a dog yet here they are, thanks to Mr Banks – or 'the Nob', as Mr Monkhouse somewhat impudently calls him. I heard the unmistakable barking as the dogs were led aboard, and I'm afraid that, unable to control myself, I did emit the unworthy exclamation 'Oh, shit'. My own concerns are affected very badly by this surprise. I had dreamed of sitting with Mr Banks and his friend Dr Solander, discussing with them the glories of the new Linnaean system of binomial classification; but these dreams are now utterly destroyed, to be replaced by the subject for a painting illustrative of the vanity of feline wishes: *The End of Clever Cat Timkins, Shaken to Death by a Nob's Greyhound on Board the Endeavour*. I have attempted to find solace in my mental store of Dr H.'s works, but I find he has written more on general moral topics, and has never come near to imagining the plight of a young cat, burning with scientific curiosity, at sea in a storm on a small bouncing boat patrolled by slavering dogs.

We are about to set sail. It is my last chance to disembark, but should I miss the adventure? Would I ever forgive myself? Also, I told family and friends not to expect me at home until at least the middle of September, and it is yet just August 26th. I suppose I can bear this for another three weeks! It has been encouraging that on the last couple of days at sea, I spewed only on the hour and not on the half-hour, and Mr Monkhouse assures me I will become a proper sailor soon, and he has fashioned a small seat for me eight feet up against the foremast, which he believes will help me not to fall ill if I look out constantly to the horizon and suck frequently on a piece of cloth soaked liberally with gin. As luck would have it, the little seat is just out of reach of the jaws of Mr Banks's dogs, however high they might jump and snap. Of course, this makes me much more of a known figure aboard the ship, but Mr Monkhouse has begun to introduce me to the crew as his cat 'Tom', and has promised the cat-hating Captain that I will never be found in the vicinity of the Great Cabin.

I have spotted a mistake in the itinerary, by the way. It says we must observe the 'Transit of Venus' from King George's Island (or Tahiti) in June! But June came and went before we even got started. I am surprised no one has spotted this and changed it!

August 29th, 1768

I have had the most disturbing conversation this morning with Mr Monkhouse. He says that we will not be home by September, and he asked me quite roughly why I ever thought we would. I cast my mind back, and it seemed to me that Dr H. had promised me a birthday tea on my return, with fish and cream and so on. 'How old be you now?' asked Mr Monkhouse, and when I said that I was two years old, he laughed and said, 'You will be five or six before you lay eyes on England again, my lad!' We were chatting in his cabin; Mr Monkhouse asked me what brought me to the ship, and I said with pride, 'Scientific curiosity,' at which he laughed and clapped his thigh, saying, 'Well, you know what they say about cats and curiosity, young Tom!' At which mysterious outburst I was about to inquire his exact meaning when with a loud barking both of Mr Banks's hounds appeared in the room and I was forced to leap for a rafter to escape them.

We will stop in Madeira. If I wish to disembark, this will be my last chance to leave the *Endeavour*'s expedition, Mr Monkhouse says. Were I to go home from Madeira, however, what will I have learned? As we have sailed south, I have been keeping my charts and I find now that the rocking of the boat, and the NOISE, and the SMELL – none of these prevents me from assessing our position, which I check against Mr Cook's own charts whenever the coast is clear and I can sneak into the Great Cabin. They cried 'Land ahoy!' when they first sighted Madeira, but I knew precisely where on the horizon the island would appear. And then, perhaps I am growing more comfortable with my maritime life! On Tuesday night, I was in my 'cat's nest', as Mr Monkhouse calls it, and as the ship sailed on straight and true under the bright stars, and I could see the planet Mars so clearly, as I had never seen it through my telescope in Bromley, and as the ship rocked gently beneath me, and creaked, and the sails flapped above my head, I not only felt happy for the first time since the voyage commenced; I also felt so strongly that dear Dr H. back at home in Bromley was thinking of me, blessing me from afar for my courage and resilience in the face of such utterly disgusting conditions. I tried not to think of his saying, 'Think of the twenty thousand pounds.' Likewise I tried not to think of the frightening gleam in his eye when he pressed upon me my sealed instructions. I preferred to remember his edifying words as he left me at the dockyard in Deptford: 'Thomas Timkins, the time is coming when all will recognise the supreme navigational cleverness of cats. Forget about the prize money. Keep a journal, my dear protégé. Follow to the letter my instructions when you reach Tahiti. On your return, you shall be famous.'

I wonder why Captain Cook is not a proper captain, yet commands the vessel? I must inquire of Mr Monkhouse why our commander has only the rank of First Lieutenant. 'Captain Cook' has such a fine ring to it. It is such a shame that he abominates cats, or I might be a welcome guest in the Great Cabin every night, where the candles blaze and there is loud merriment brought on by wine and rum. By the bye, Mr Monkhouse's idea of aiding my nausea by way of gin has been such a great success that I drink this excellent spirit now at every opportunity. I find it calms the nerves. When I return to London they will hardly know me, such a rough-and-tough nautical cat will I have become! Mr Monkhouse looks after me with great kindness and insists that my ability to conduct scientific conversations should be kept a secret until the time is right. I keep meaning to ask when he thinks the time will be right, but I keep forgetting, and then I nod off on account of all the gin!

September 18th, 1768

I was not expecting a bullock on board, but the gin helps take the edge off most surprises, I find. Oh, look, we've got a bullock now as well, I thought to myself yesterday, as we prepared to sail from Madeira, and instead of demanding to know where the bullock was supposed to *go* and what it was going to *eat* and what was to be done with its *dung*, I just lapped from my bowl and felt a cheering warmth flood through my paws and ears. Mr Banks and his company took the dogs ashore, thank goodness; they returned later with botanical specimens and exotic fruits that I yearned desperately to see. While the company were ashore, I took the opportunity to inspect Mr Banks's journal, which is full of birds and fish he has observed; I felt ashamed that I had seen so little, and that my knowledge of natural history is so small. I did not take this last opportunity to leave the ship for good. Mr Monkhouse offered to take me ashore, and so was I set down on dry land after a full two months aboard the *Endeavour*, and it was a horrible sensation as the ground rose up to hit me, and I shook from head to tail. 'Was there an earthquake?' I asked Mr Monkhouse, and he laughed and said I had better remain on board, at which he tucked me into his own bed and left me to sleep there in the relative quiet of the new-provisioned ship.

September 20th, 1768

There is one aspect of Mr Banks's project of collecting that I had not anticipated. Every day, it seems, he spots something new in nature and then he kills it, and I am beginning to find this custom morally questionable, not to say abhorrent. Today they caught a 'Medusa' – a magnificent sea creature – and as they hauled it aboard, I watched from my cat's nest with tears rolling down my face! Being a man of science myself I know I should be dispassionate. But whenever I have ventured to the Great Cabin, what I have seen there is, first, beautiful paintings of the living beasts by the artist Mr Parkinson, and then also smelly, bloody bits of birds and fish and animals that have been dissected by Mr Banks and Dr Solander. As a fellow of the London Lunar Society I applaud their tireless application of themselves to the classification of the natural world, but when I see a sea creature dragged from its element to its evident great distress, I feel no triumph, only pity and remorse.

I have been thinking, these last few days, of a conversation that took place between myself and Mr Hodge on the eve of my embarkation. I hesitate to set it down. These last weeks at sea I have striven hard to forget his words; to push them to the anterior of my mind. Mr Hodge, I should explain, has lived for several years under the roof of Dr Samuel Johnson, and he is our Lunar Society's greatest ornament. A classicist, a great stylist and a splendid poet, Mr Hodge is rumoured to be the true author of the recently discovered poems of 'Ossian' which many, including Dr Johnson, believe to be the work of an ancient bard! I am very much in awe of Mr Hodge; his opinion carries great weight with me. That there was once a close friendship between our two dear doctors is acknowledged on both sides. That they have fallen out of friendship I also know, but the cause is not hard to find. My dear Dr H. has been rewarded for his efforts, where Dr Johnson, so often, has not. Envy is an unworthy emotion; it is one of the seven deadly sins; and one hesitates to adduce it. Yet surely sheer unworthy jealousy is at the root of their discord?

It was at the end of the last meeting of the Society that Mr Hodge asked me to walk with him down Fetter Lane towards the Thames. I happily acceded but I will never forget the shock of his first words.

'Beware John Hawkesworth, young Timkins,' he said. 'Behind your back, he despises you.'

I remember that it took a short while for me to consider what he was saying.

'Sir, you are wrong,' I replied hotly. 'He is not only a good man, he is famous for his excellent judgment, rectitude and elevated sentiments. His very doctor's degree was conferred upon him by the Archbishop of Canterbury in recognition of his many personal merits as reflected in his essays.'

'I say nothing to his skill as a writer,' replied Hodge, 'or indeed his unerring ability of expressing such thoughts that gratify popular attitudes. I speak of his character regarding his friends. Have you not observed how he treats his old friend Dr Johnson?'

I was relieved that it was on this familiar but thorny matter that Mr Hodge's opinion rested.

'Your master is simply envious of Dr Hawkesworth,' I said, complacent. 'Have *you* not observed, sir, that Dr Johnson's journal *The*

Rambler attracted far less pecuniary reward than Dr Hawkesworth's *Adventurer*? In the theatre, Dr Hawkesworth's play at Drury Lane attained more performances than Dr Johnson's. His Oriental tales have been more warmly received and have found more wealthy admirers than Dr Johnson's *Rasselas*. When he succeeded Dr Johnson as composer of parliamentary debates in the *Gentleman's Magazine*, his papers were generally accorded better than Johnson's because he did not employ such ridiculous long words.'

At this last point, Mr Hodge drew breath to reply, but I had not finished.

'Dr H.,' I went on, 'also rejoices in a spacious house and a very nice wife, neither of which comforts does Dr Johnson possess. I agree that it is hard for a friendship to endure between men whose literary paths lie so close to one another's yet differ so widely in degree of pecuniary reward, but it is unfair to traduce Dr Hawkesworth's character on account of his having the greater name and better living than those of his erstwhile friend.'

It was a long speech and I was proud of it. Especially the grammar, which in parts was quite complex.

Hodge held up a paw. 'Are you not aware, young Timkins,' he demanded, 'what is generally said of Dr Hawkesworth's style?'

'Yes,' I said proudly. 'That it is almost indistinguishable from Dr Johnson's.'

'Not the other way round?'

'Pardon?'

'The model is Johnson; the imitator is Hawkesworth.'

'Well, yes. But the word imitator is surely ill-chosen.'

'Did Dr Hawkesworth write the debates before Johnson or after?'

What was he getting at now?

'Well, after.'

'Did he write his periodical before *The Rambler* or after it?'

'After it, but—'

'And the Oriental tales, and the play?'

'Both after. But he is younger than Dr Johnson!'

My head was in some confusion. Dear Dr H. did not deserve these insinuations.

'You know your master had no proper schooling,' Hodge went on. 'That he is ignorant of the classics?'

'Yes, and he is to be congratulated for overcoming such a lamentable disadvantage,' I said.

'His father was a watch-chaser. Some people say a watch-*maker*, but the difference is eloquent. Hawkesworth's father did not *make* watches, he merely *improved them for sale*.'

I could take no more. 'Mr Hodge, please explain why you are telling me this. It hurts me very much to hear such bad opinion of my dear doctor. He is the Cat Master, after all. We owe him loyalty and thanks. The Cat Master would do nothing to harm any of us. We bask in his good nature!'

Hodge looked upon me pityingly.

'Has it not struck you,' he asked, 'that there is nothing in Scripture concerning Cat Masters, Timkins? Dr Johnson asked me to inquire into Cat Master history, when he was offered the post himself. There is nothing in the Torah, the Testaments, the Apocrypha. The post itself dates back less than one hundred years. You do know that Sir Henry Fielding desired for Dr Johnson to be his successor, but Dr Johnson declined it?'

'No!' I said.

'Oh yes. Dr Johnson declined the post. He said the smell of sulphur was attached to it, and I believe that he was right.'

'Nonsense.'

'And I would point out to you, and ask you to consider, that all your dear doctor's wholly undeserved worldly success has come to him *since he became Cat Master*.'

Again, I was simply shocked that Hodge should speak so wickedly. Did he now accuse Dr H. of being in league with the Devil?

'I must leave you here,' I said stiffly. 'I board the *Endeavour* in the next few days.' And then I broke down. 'Why are you making these slanderous accusations, Mr Hodge?' I wailed.

'Don't go on the ship,' he said. 'If Hawkesworth has offered you fame—'

'He hasn't!' I sobbed.

'If he has offered you fame,' Mr Hodge repeated, 'do not believe him. He forgets his friends when he needs them no longer. He is a monster of ambition. I heard my dear Dr Johnson say the other day that "*Dr Hawkesworth is grown a coxcomb, and I have done with him.*" He said to another, "*Sir, if you should ever entertain the sensation of having been climbed, it is a sign you have met with Dr Hawkesworth."'*

'I am sorry Dr Johnson says such things,' I said. 'But is it not possible that he is envious of—'

He cut me short. He was angry now. 'Envious? Envious of what? Tell me one memorable thing that your dear doctor has ever written or said that could make Dr Johnson envious!'

But he didn't wait to hear my practised recitation of *Adventurer CXL*, in which the great man writes that 'Vice is a gradual and easy descent, where it first deviates from the level of innocence; but the declivity at every pace becomes more steep, and those who descend, descend every moment with greater rapidity.'

He left me to my thoughts. And I walked on, alone.

September 24th, 1768

Today we saw flying fish! Fish that fly! To a cat, this was almost unbearably exciting. One of them flew on to the deck, and before the men of science could come forward with their scalpels and drawing boards, I'm afraid to say I tore it to pieces and ate it. How the crew laughed and cheered at Mr Banks's disappointment! Outwitted by a cat! I was very pleased myself, I must declare. Tenerife was later sighted, but of course I knew it was coming, so I could not share in the general surprise.

October 3rd, 1768

We have lost the trade winds, and the *Endeavour* idles in the water, which means Mr Banks and his party can take their small boat and murder more exotic sea creatures. The ship is very damp.

October 18th, 1768

Today Mr Monkhouse was called to attend on Mr Banks. Mr B., attempting to exercise on deck with a pair of ropes, it seems tripped over and hit his head. Mr Monkhouse, knowing how much I longed to know what scientific discoveries have yet been made, made request that the dogs be chained elsewhere for the duration of his medical examination, and took me therefore safely with him to Mr Banks's sleeping quarters to the side of the Great Cabin. He set me down and gave me half an hour to prowl around; I was in very heaven. First, I checked that Dr H.'s sealed instructions were still safe in the little cupboard, which they were, although I noted that the ink on the outer leaf had faded somewhat, and that it was hard to read my name. What did I care for this, however, when I might, in this little room, allow myself to revel in the sheer light of reason, without which I had languished these past few weeks. Such infinite riches in this little room! Light itself was all around, thanks to the elegant windows. Books lay all about. Dr Solander was at the table, making notes, Mr Parkinson drawing and painting with great speed and accuracy; one of the servants feeding insects to a small yellow bird – a *Motacilla avida*, according to the labelled watercolour lying close by – that evidently flew on to the ship four weeks ago and is being kept as a pet by Mr Banks. Of course my presence was noted – and not entirely kindly. Dr Solander said, 'Most we haff zis cat in ze room?' But Mr Parkinson patted me on the head. I was careful to show no interest in the bird and kept well away from it (they have not forgotten the flying fish!), but I could not help sighing aloud at this vision of industry. When Mr Monkhouse collected me and returned me to the darkness and stuffiness of the lower deck, I waited until he had left and then I curled up in a ball and sobbed.

October 21st, 1768

I am accused of murder! This morning I could contain myself no longer. While Mr Monkhouse was again attending Mr Banks (whose head is better), and the Great Cabin was for once deserted, I was overwhelmed by desire to see what Mr Parkinson was doing, so I hopped up on to the table at exactly the same moment – oh luckless Timkins! – that the little yellow bird hopped down upon it. 'I beg your pardon,' I said to it. And then I said, 'Are you all right?' because the bird had fallen on its side and did not appear to be breathing. The way its lifeless beady eyes looked at me unnerved me quite. Of course I felt very sorry it had died (of shock, no doubt), but I had no idea that these men who dissect and destroy life day after day would feel so strongly about the demise of this one little bird. Mr Banks, on entering the room, was furious. 'What have you done to that beautiful innocent wagtail?' he thundered. I felt this was a bit rich, coming from him, and was about to say so but Mr Monkhouse swept me away, making all sorts of unnecessary apologies and promising I would never be allowed into this part of the ship again. I am in despair. Mr Banks hates me! He thinks

I am the sort of cat who kills for sport! Worse, my natural place on the ship will now never, ever be mine.

October 25th, 1768

I will never forgive those bastards for this. I will never forgive them, not as long as I live. Have I mental powers enough to relate all that has happened? I fear not! I fear my heart will break! But oh, dear Lord, I must set this down and for ever after when men speak high of Joseph Banks and Captain Cook, I shall know the truth of these men by what was done to me this day.

Today we crossed the Equator. I must confess I was interested in recording the moment of our crossing; in particular I wanted to observe whether water truly stops swirling in one direction and starts swirling in the opposite direction, due to magnetic differences north and south of this imaginary line. No one had told me of the ceremonies and traditions that are observed in this wooden world to celebrate the crossing. Certainly no one told me that all the crew who had not crossed before, *including dogs and cats,* were to be dunked in the sea. The whole company being gathered on deck, a roll call of those qualifying for the ritual was read aloud, and it included all of Mr Banks's party; also Captain Cook; also those horrible dogs; also me. The forfeit for not being dunked is to give up one's share of rum; being more of a gin man myself, I was therefore stuck. Mr Banks paid up with sufficient spirituous drink to excuse himself, all of his party, also Captain Cook, also the dogs. But when it came to saving me, he decided against it. 'That cat killed my wagtail,' he said. 'Let it sink or swim.'

I ran and hid in the hold. I was discovered and dragged out, amidst much cheering. Mr Monkhouse offered to pay for me, but they would not listen! And then, one by one, the men were attached to a wooden plank and lowered into the sea! As my turn approached, all I could think of was Mr Tinkle's wig falling on the floor just as he lifted his leg to micturate: up to this point, it had been for me the strongest instance of cat humiliation I had known – of a cat over-reaching himself and being mocked by fate. How much worse was this! Curiosity would kill this cat, after all, just as Mr Monkhouse had predicted.

Neither he nor his brother – the midshipman – were to be dunked, having crossed the Equator on other occasions, but just as my name was called aloud, 'Tom the Surgeon's Cat, step forward!', the brother stepped up fully clothed. I had no idea what was going on. Was he rescuing me? Was he proposing to jump over the side and swim a thousand miles to the nearest shore? No, he was volunteering to undertake the ordeal along of me! Picking me up he said, 'It won't be as bad as you think.' Then he allowed himself to be tied to the plank, and he held me tight inside his blue jacket, and then whoa! We were plummeting downwards, head first, with him saying, 'Don't breathe! Close your eyes!' then striking the surface of the waves and the water – so much water! – filling our ears and pressing on us and enclosing us. How I wriggled and scratched poor Jonathan Monkhouse! The sensation of being under water – of being dragged through water by the movement of the ship – was beyond any endurance, and I fought him even though he was trying to help me. Then we were raised, dripping and gasping, and he said, 'Just let it happen, it will soon end.' Then we were dunked again, and then a third time, at which point Mr Jonathan said, 'That's it, well done.' And we both did start to relax, because three dunkings was the proper number. But on Banks's express command (as we later discovered), we were then dunked a fourth time, when we were unprepared, and I drank in so much salt water that I could breathe no air after, and I was sure that I would die.

Mr Monkhouse broke the news to me this evening that he was not joking when he said I would be five or six years old before we see England again. By current reckoning, we will not reach Tahiti until next June; after the astronomical experiment has been completed there, we will not, even then, go home. Captain Cook has secret orders (which everyone except me seems to know about) to stay at sea in the *Endeavour* until he finds the so-called 'Southern Continent'. The terrible truth is that I might have to stay on this fucking, fucking ship for at least the next three years.

Document Two

Proceedings of the London Lunar Society,
reconvened in its 262nd year
with its original members

(notes taken by Mr Nolly in haste;
to be polished at a later date if necessary)

HERE present:

Mr Andrewes
Mr Buzz
Mr Bruise
Mr Scratchy

Mr Oliver (Nolly)
Mr Tinkle
Mr MacJockie
Mr Cuddles
Mr Hawkins
Sr Andreotti
Mrs Stella
As always, a chair was set for Mr Timkins, *in absentia*

Mr Andrewes delivered to the assembled society the following information, which did make us sore depressed and make some of us wonder and even cry aloud in distress why we have bothered to stay alive for *a quarter of a millennium*, if in the end, when the chips were down, we could execute so little of our long-made plans.

ONE. *The diverse diggings in the Bromley churchyard by the old woman FLETCHER and the Female Kitten of Uncouth Accent, which we did as a group forcefully oppose and strive to prevent, have been successful.*

General consternation. Although our extraordinary longevity was not, to be strict, our own choice (being imposed upon us all by the Cat Master in those far-off Enlightenment days), it has been agreed among us always that at least it was worthwhile, since through our faithful vigilance the world would be safe from that which was buried all those years ago. Mr Nolly enquiring if the excavated idol had been actually seen by any of the society, Mr Andrewes replied he had seen it plainly in the hands of the old woman Fletcher, and it had made him quake. Even more consternation, and general shivering in horror, Mr Buzz indeed needing to be revived after fainting. Mr Bruise, in his frustration, punched a hole in the wall. Out of delicacy and long friendship, I will not here name the gentleman who by accident did micturate upon the floor, but it was the same gentleman who, in long-ago happier times, famously pissed on his own wig.

Mr MacJockie said he would like to take this opportunity to speak at length on the subject of scientific enquiry redounding not always to the benefit of mankind. He had been preparing a few thoughts on this subject for the past two hundred years. General shaking of heads and muttering of 'What, *now*?' and 'MacJock doesn't change much, does he?' *et cetera, et cetera.* Mr Bruise offering to 'knock his block off'; the rest of us declining.

Mr Andrewes replied to Mr MacJockie that at present there was much to be done, and that just as Mr MacJockie had had hundreds of years to prepare his thoughts on this subject, he had likewise had hundreds of years in which to deliver them. Mutterings of 'hear, hear'. A vote was taken. All agreed that Mr MacJockie should save his philosophical remarks for another occasion. MacJockie accepted the feelings of the group, but spent the rest of the meeting with his tail curled tightly round him and his face in such a scowl that his whiskers stood almost vertical, but we are well accustomed to this sour expression and accordingly took no notice.

TWO. *The old woman Fletcher and the Female Kitten of Uncouth Accent are in possession of Timkins's journal.*

General dismay. We have been trying to locate Timkins's journal since 1773. We now suspect it was buried along of Dr Hawkesworth, with the idol.

THREE. *Our attempt to murder the old woman Fletcher and the Female Kitten of Uncouth Accent by purring their house down was in some respects a triumph, and a significant tribute to the late lamented Mr Hodge, whose calculations, diagrams and detailed elevations were of great utility in the enterprise. However, the old woman and the monstrous kitten being away from home when we did perform the purring, it was not only a wasted effort but set us back in our attempts to contain the idol, as we now don't know where it is. We have also lost the element of surprise.*

Much groaning and slapping of foreheads. Mr MacJockie said (of course) that he had opposed the purring experiment all along. Mr Buzz said Mr MacJockie was always thus wise after the event, wasn't he; Mr Scratchy suggested a catfight, there and then, to settle matters; Mr MacJockie said och, we'd really like that, wouldn't we; Mr Tinkle excused himself for the usual reason; Mrs Stella appealed for calm; Mr Bruise punched a hole in another wall; and the meeting threatening to break up in violence until Mr Andrewes called us all to order and demanded apologies from everyone present *including me*, and I'd had nothing to do with it, and I said so quite hotly, but in the interests of calm I acceded, and we could go on.

FOUR. *A new member proposed by Mr Andrewes.*

General confusion. How can we admit new members, after all this time? What new members could there possibly be? Mr Andrewes reported he had been approached by a certain learned and persuasive cat, regrettably having no wig to his name, who had only lately learned of our continued existence. Mr Andrewes assured him that though we met less frequently than of old, we were proud of our Lunar brotherhood, and that we were bound by shared feelings of undying devotion towards the outrageously under-celebrated Dr Hawkesworth.

Said cat was excellently well qualified, having read wide in the classics, and also being 'a wiz on the Internet', whatever those words may signify. He also intimated to Mr Andrewes the stupendous and wholly unexpected news that he had, until recently, been 'intimately acquainted with poor Timkins'.

This was astonishing, and we were all suspicious. 'What does that mean?' demanded Mr Scratchy. 'How could he have been acquainted with Timkins? Does he mean acquainted with his story?' At this point, Mr Tinkle returned to the room and was apprised of what had happened. He averred it was very unlikely that anyone would claim to have known Timkins. All groaned their agreement. Poor Timkins was lost to us so long ago! As Mr Nolly said (although Mrs Stella says she said it too),

Timkins came back from that voyage a very changed cat indeed. Gone was the gentleness; gone the spark. His burps alone were so prodigious and alcoholic that several of us were rendered unconscious by their spirituous content. What he had suffered on that voyage was beyond all our imaginings.

Mr Andrewes shrugged. He was ever one of the best shruggers in the clever cat community. Continuing to describe the surprising applicant for fellowship: 'He says he knew Timkins much later, meeting him in – when was it?' He consulted his notes. 'He met him in 1927 in the East End of London. By then, poor Timkins went by the name "the Captain". But he told this cockney cat his full story, apparently – the same story that, on his immediate return from Cook's voyage, he could not bear to tell to us.'

'Where is Timkins now?' Mr Nolly enquired, daring to ask the question that all were secretly thinking. The empty chair had drawn all eyes.

'I believe he is dead,' said Mr Andrewes, his voice cracking a little. 'Just three years since. Deliberately stripped of his powers – the ones conferred on him, and us all, by Dr Hawkesworth – he was drowned down a well in Dorset.'

At this, all shuddered and closed their eyes, but Mr Nolly did not weep at all, or shake with secret sobs, whatever anyone else might tell you. He merely looked at the floor for a while, and continued to make notes. However, Mr Nolly having been a special friend to Timkins in the early days of the Society, it would have been perfectly understandable if he *had* given way to emotion. A quarter of a millennium is a long time to wait (in hope) to hear if your best friend is alive or dead.

'Will this new member help us with recovering the idol?' asked Mr Tinkle, who then with a look of mortification said, 'Oh no, not again,' and fled the room to attend to other business.

'This is, I believe, Mr Roger's sole purpose in joining us,' replied Mr Andrewes. 'And I think we should admit him as soon as possible. I received the impression that Mr Roger not only has experience of facing evil at close quarters; he is also unbelievably *clever*.'

A vote was taken on the admission of Mr Roger, which was unanimous if you don't count Mr MacJockie, who was sulking as usual and refused to take part. Mrs Stella said she would happily explain what the Internet was, if anyone was interested, but we decided there was no time. We concluded our meeting in the traditional manner with a group yowl lasting several minutes, not because it was quite the full moon yet, but because Sr Andreotti has no other function in the group than to lead us in our yowling, and it felt wrong on so momentous an occasion to leave him altogether outside of the proceedings.

Document Three

Application for One-to-One Meeting with Beelzebub First-time applicants only

Please give all information as truthfully as your natural wicked deviousness permits. We do understand this is difficult for the truly evil, but we request that you try.

Please avoid exclamation marks, as His Darkness feels very strongly on the subject of redundant punctuation.

Please note that all questions with an ✡ attract a surcharge.

1. Name
Tetty

1a. Any aliases
Kitty, Kittikins, Ronetta Kray

2. Species
Cat

2a. Any subspecies
Evil talking

3. Age (real)
Fifty-nine

3a. Age (apparent)
Eight weeks

4. Nature of business
Restoration of post of Cat Master, but with me in control; in return, gift of priceless evil Tahitian idol 'Oviri' to Beelzebub

5. Do you require the presence of the Devil and all his demons? *
No

6. Do you require catering? *
No

7. Do you require flames and other effects? *
(Please note: red smoke is non-negotiable. His Darkness never works without it.)
No

8. Give desired date and time for this meeting
Midnight of Wednesday, 24 December (full moon)

9. Give desired meeting place
23 Chislehurst Gardens, Bromley

10. Are there any parking difficulties?
No

11. Any desired location at this address? Bear in mind His Darkness does not manifest in kitchens, lofts or garden sheds
The living room, if possible

12. How grateful to Beelzebub will you be for this, on a scale of one to ten?
Ten

12a. If you answered 'ten' to the above question, please answer the following:

Do you deliver your immortal soul to him in perpetuity?
Yes

Do you understand the expressions 'immortal soul' and 'perpetuity'?
Yes

Do you accept there is no 'cooling-off period' to this contract?
Yes

13. Given the extreme pressure placed upon His Darkness, and his absolute fury at sometimes turning up and finding no one waiting for him, please answer the following question pertaining to your request:

Are you a time-waster?
No.

Thank you for your interest. There are many people requiring the services of Beelzebub at present, and we require ten working days to process each request.

It is now our policy to charge half your immortal soul as a down payment, to be retained by us in case of a no-show. Please tick box to agree to these terms and conditions. ☑

If you are a human, please supply email address

If you are a cat, please supply e-miaow address
tetty@eviltalkingcat.demon.co.uk

Please make no plans until you have heard from us. Requests are currently running at less than a 2% success rate. We apologise for making you fill in the entire form and then telling you this discouraging news right at the end.

One last question. His Darkness has desired us to ask this of every single applicant for the past 250 years:

14. Have you ever heard of/seen/handled an object called the OVIRI? Or do you have it now?
Yes! See above, question 4!

If by any chance your answer to the above question is 'Yes', and you are willing to give it up, there is a strong possibility you will not only be successful in your request but also reign alongside His Darkness throughout the rest of time.

Please sign below. Paw prints accepted.

Your ref number is 347891IMI15F4300P3232 XX32666

Please quote this number in all correspondence.

Part Three

Chapter Four

It took very little time to get to Bromley. I don't know why I had previously been so resistant to making this journey; perhaps I'd got it mixed up with Bournemouth in my head. Wiggy, it turned out, knew Bromley well from the theatre circuit, and had considerable affection for the town; on the way there, possibly to distract my thoughts from the horrific thing that had been done to my body by the demon kitten Tetty, he talked of some of the plays he'd been in – many of them murder mysteries in which he (Wiggy) had played an early victim. Early victim seemed to be a speciality of Wiggy's. Often, he explained, he was dead before the interval, but sometimes he was dead within the first ten minutes. 'I actually prefer to be the first to go,' he said (and it was hard to tell if he was just being brave about this). 'The thing is, if you go at the start, it's a bit more shocking for the audience. They care more. And of course, once I'm off I get to crack open the wine in the dressing rooms and get started on the party!'

On arrival, we checked into a venerable hotel near the church. From the look of it, it had once been a coaching inn. Then I called the vet's for a report on Watson (he was now perfectly well, they said, but they could 'tell he was missing me'), and then Wiggy and I had an argument over whether I should report to the nearest A & E department, to show them my foot. We had very different views on this. Wiggy's opinion was that if you've got a moist, red-lipped, repulsive little gaping hole on your ankle, you should try to get it seen to. By contrast, I thought that if you simply ignored it, it might go away. I was pleased to find that the numbness had passed, and I no longer hobbled. Less happily, we had discovered that if (experimentally) you placed a finger lightly against the little soft lips, they reacted to the pressure by sucking.

'Perhaps they'll know what it is,' Wiggy kept saying. 'At A & E.'

'Of course they won't, Wiggy.'

We were walking to the parish church at the time, to see for ourselves where the 'abominations' had taken place. For once, it wasn't raining. A tall, bedraggled Christmas tree stood outside.

Wiggy wouldn't give up on the hospital theme. 'They might say, "Oh, we've seen this many times before, Mr Charlesworth. It's *mouthey-mouthey-itis*, there's a lot of it about."'

'"*Mouthey-mouthey-itis*"?' I repeated. 'Wiggy, please stop.'

He tried to reply, but I talked over him. 'Look, if it *is* something called "*mouthey-mouthey-itis*", and there's "a lot of it about", then I don't need to worry, do I? If, on the other hand, it's more to do with something quite specific, such as that it's the curse of a malevolent idol of South Sea origins possibly dating from the second half of the eighteenth century, I think our best course of action is to stay on its trail, and not spend twelve hours in a waiting room with blood smears on the lino until a very tired man in a white jacket finally takes a look at it and shouts, "Oh my God, what the fuck is that? The bloody thing just sucked my finger!"' My voice had risen. I lowered it. 'Besides, Wiggy, we know we've only got till tomorrow's full moon to sort all this out.'

Wiggy stopped.

'Sorry, tomorrow's what? How do we know that?'

'Tetty. She said something about "him" coming on Wednesday, at the full moon. Christmas Eve, as it happens.'

'Oh yes.'

We walked on.

'And today is Tuesday,' I said.

'Right. Yes.'

We had by now arrived at the churchyard, which looked smaller and less atmospheric than it had done on television. In fact, it looked completely unremarkable now that the incident tape had been taken down, and the excavations had been filled in. I was quite disappointed. We agreed we should have a look at Hawkesworth's tomb inside the church, and were just about to go inside when Wiggy made a proposal sensationally ill-advised.

'Alec, can I do it again?' he said.

To his credit, he did seem a bit sheepish when he said this. I remember hoping that he didn't mean what I thought he meant.

'What do you mean? What would you like to do?' I said carefully.

He lowered his voice. 'Touch the whatsit again. The mouthey-mouthey thing. Just to check.'

'What? You're joking. It's probably got teeth by now.'

'No. Go on.'

'Really? You realise what any passing Freudian psychoanalyst would make of this – your asking if you can touch my mouthey-mouthey thing?'

'Ah,' he said, 'but are there likely to be any Freudian psychoanalysts passing by at this hour, Alec?'

I sighed. And I will never forgive myself: instead of flatly refusing, I said all right. So we sat down together on a little bench and, checking first that there was no one in sight, I offered him the offending ankle and tried to look the other way.

'I'd just like to put on record that this was not my idea,' I said.

'I know!' he said brightly.

Then he put the back of his right hand against the little mouth, waited a few seconds, and pulled a face.

'Nothing,' he said, as if disappointed.

'Good,' I said. 'Then perhaps—'

But then, just as he pulled his hand away, it was sucked back with such violent force ('Woah!') that it became quite tightly stuck.

'All right, that's enough,' I said. 'Pull away now.'

But Wiggy didn't pull away, because he couldn't.

'Oh, come on,' he said in disbelief, standing up, with his arm at a tricky angle. And then his face contorted as the skin on his hand was drawn tighter.

'Ow!' he shouted. 'OW! OW! OW!'

When I think back on this, I expect the whole episode to be accompanied by a loud industrial Hoover-type noise to represent the force of the suction coming from my ankle – but it was silent. Appallingly silent.

'Alec, do something!' he shouted.

'It's not me,' I said. 'I'm not doing it.'

'Help!' he yelled.

'Pull harder,' I said. 'Harder!'

It was at this moment that the vicar appeared round the corner of the church, chatting to an elderly lady parishioner in a mauve hat, and found Wiggy and me engaged in some sort of perverted wrestling activity in broad daylight on a bench, with Wiggy panting heavily, 'This is incredible!' and me yelling, 'Harder, for God's sake. Harder!'

On spotting the vicar, Wiggy manfully controlled himself, and I put my foot to the ground, so Wiggy's hand went with it, and we had to pretend he was tying his shoelace.

We both tried to look normal. Sweat broke out on Wiggy's face. He was obviously in considerable discomfort.

'Good morning,' said the vicar, stopping. 'Are you in difficulties?'

I laughed. 'Heavens, no,' I said.

'No, no,' said Wiggy, a bit muffled. 'Damn shoelace.'

'I had the impression you were in difficulties.'

'No, no,' we both said. 'No, not at all, no.'

Wiggy looked up, which wasn't easy. His face was contorted with pain, but he managed a smile.

'Happy Christmas,' he said, as brightly as he possibly could.

Obviously we expected the vicar to move on, but he didn't. Instead, he peered at Wiggy's face, and seemed to recognise him.

'Pardon me for asking, but weren't you recently at the Churchill Theatre in the cast of *And Then There Were None*?'

It is a mark of any actor that, even when he is bent double with the back of his hand stuck painfully tight to a supernatural oral aperture sprouting from the left ankle of his best friend, he will still be absolutely delighted when someone asks a question like this.

'Gosh, yes,' he said with gritted teeth. 'I played the young chap who'd murdered some bally children by running them over in a fast car.'

I joined in, to draw attention away from Wiggy for a second. 'I didn't see it, I'm afraid. But I'm sure he was very good.'

The vicar leaned in. 'Excellent projectile vomiting, right off the stage,' he explained to me. 'As I can attest at first hand, having been in the front row!'

I glanced at the woman next to the vicar, and we both laughed politely. Everyone looked down to where Wiggy's hand was stuck – and then suddenly he was released, and he sat up smartly, covering the affected right hand with his left, and I moved my foot, and Wiggy chuckled, 'Well, thanks so much for coming.'

The vicar beamed.

'I hope it washed off,' added Wiggy. 'It was only beans and stuff.'

'Oh yes,' said the vicar. 'Eventually.'

'We would never use real vomit.'

'How reassuring.'

He and the woman finally decided to continue their walk, and we said goodbye. When they were safely round a corner, Wiggy's face crumpled.

'Oh my *God*,' he wailed. He revealed the hand, which was purple and black with bruises. He tried to flex the fingers, but the effort made him wince so much that he stopped, and groaned. I took a peek at the mouthey-mouthey thing. It was wet with some sort of saliva, and it seemed to have grown.

'That was jolly decent of him,' he said at last.

'Yes,' I agreed. 'Especially as you'd spattered him with puke.'

'It was mentioned in quite a lot of the reviews,' he said. 'Not being sick on the vicar; just the being sick. All done with a little pipe that I held up to my chin with cupped hands.'

It seemed a shame to call a halt to this pleasant digression about simulated vomit, but I felt I must. 'Wiggy, do *you* want to go to A & E now?'

'No, no, I'm all right,' he said, putting the injured hand in his pocket. 'And anyway, we ought to follow that woman, actually; there's not a moment to lose.'

'Why? That wasn't Mrs Fletcher,' I said.

'No, I know that. But didn't you notice the smell?'

I shook my head. 'What smell?'

'Alec, she smelled of stew!'

'Did she?'

'I suppose I got more of a whiff of her when I was bent over,' he said. 'Come on.'

We rose and walked briskly (despite our injuries) to where we had last seen the woman with the mauve hat disappear with the vicar. She was still in sight. Having separated from her companion, she was now making her way to the high street.

I sniffed the air, not expecting to pick anything up, but I did. It was faint but definite. A mixture of meat stew, incense, and Parma violets.

'Well done, Wiggy. We must follow that woman,' I said.

But we did not follow her. Because, just as I was opening the gate, a voice behind us said, 'It's all right, there's no need; I know where she's going: twenty-three Chislehurst Gardens.' And we looked round, and emerging from behind a bush was Roger.

And so began the most extraordinary and harrowing few hours of my life. I doubt I shall ever hear the name of Bromley again without shuddering. Here in pretty eighteenth-century Bromley, Dr John Hawkesworth was buried in this country churchyard with a South Sea idol at his side, and from that time onwards, a pall of insipient evil had hung about the district. Bromley might have been twinned with an obscure town in the Rhineland (I just looked this up), but my feeble point is this: by rights it should have been twinned with Matavai Bay in Tahiti, where, in 1769, the talented young artist Sydney Parkinson from HM Bark *Endeavour* ſirst discovered and stole the Oviri, and ſateſully took it back to the ship.

Roger, of course, knew the full story. He always does. He also revels in telling stories in the right order, without leaving anything out. For once, I didn't care. I wanted to hear all of it. But first:

'How long will the full story take this time, Roger?' I asked him, as if casually.

'It will take four hours and seventeen minutes without interruptions,' he said. 'So my suggestion is that we reconvene at your hotel this evening at six thirty. Expect a number of others to be present. They deserve to hear the full story too.'

'Others?' said Wiggy.

Roger looked at me. He made me look him in the eye. He seemed to be inviting me to make a mental leap.

'Do you mean . . . the Lunar cats?' I said.

'What?' said Wiggy.

'Yes!' said Roger, pleased. 'The Lunar cats.'

Looking back, I'm quite proud that I jumped to this connection when there had been, thus far, so little explanation of things. But if there was one thing I was learning about these cat stories involving Roger, it was this: you just have to trust, in the end, that everything will be connected.

Wiggy put his head to one side. He was obviously about to say that the Lunar cats – so far as we knew – were a phenomenon of the late eighteenth century. Roger didn't let him.

'So,' Roger said, 'expect some Lunar cats. If you could provide a few saucers of milk; a spot of smoked salmon; perhaps some of those little crunchy biscuits?'

Wiggy sighed. 'You don't change much, Roger.'

'Ah, but you wouldn't want me to.'

He turned to go, but Wiggy stopped him. 'How did you survive falling down the well? And how did you get out again?'

Roger looked at both of us and said, 'I can't tell you. I wish I could. When I regained consciousness, I was on a noisy Greek ferry, behind a heap of suitcases, heading towards Symi in the Dodecanese. I have my suspicions about who saved me, but since the full story would take around two days, I suggest we save it for another occasion.'

I felt swindled. So did Wiggy. However, neither of us dared to object.

'But as regards our present difficulties,' said Roger, 'I promise I will tell you everything I can when we meet tonight. And then we must make our plan. Tomorrow night will be the full moon.'

'I know,' I said. 'Tetty said so.'

'I was so impressed that you called her Tetty, by the way,' Roger said – for once allowing himself a digression. I blushed with pleasure. Any compliment from Roger is an honour – and I'd had two in a row!

'I don't know why I did,' I admitted. 'It just came to me.'

On hearing this, Roger evidently changed his mind about the compliment. 'Of course!' he said. 'She will have hypnotised you.'

'Really?'

'Oh yes.'

'So it wasn't my idea at all?'

'Probably not. I mean, the chances are very remote of its being a coincidence. Tetty was the name the Captain gave her too, you see. He knew of the original Tetty Johnson, because she was a great friend of the Hawkesworths. I expect you know she was buried here, in this churchyard.'

'But Tetty the kitten is not an eighteenth-century cat, is she?' I said. 'She doesn't sound like one.'

'No, no. She was one of John Seeward's experiments in the 1950s, when the Captain was with him at Harville Manor. She was one of the most dangerous and creative criminal minds he produced there. You know the Hatton Garden safety deposit box raid in 2015? The one that was dubbed the perfect crime? Where they tunnelled through the wall in the basement over the bank holiday weekend?'

'Er, yes.'

'Tetty's paw prints were all over that.'

This took a moment to sink in.

'But a lot of old-codger felons were convicted for that job, weren't they?'

'Precisely. That's what makes her so good.'

'So she's a 1950s evil talking kitten?'

'That's right. Tetty was devoted to Seeward, and to his successor, Prideaux. And to the Captain. She is totally evil. She is single-handedly trying to revive the cult of the Cat Master, and to this end she has stolen your pamphlet and also – much more worryingly – unearthed the Oviri, which she intends to present to Beelzebub tomorrow night. Is this clear?'

Wiggy's eyes swivelled with alarm as he tried to take this in. I made an inward promise I would repeat it to him when Roger had departed.

'Absolutely,' I said.

Roger continued. 'The Lunar cats, by contrast, are well-intentioned Enlightenment gentlefolk who have been dedicated to preventing the Oviri from ever seeing daylight again. When Tetty's nocturnal diggings first began in the churchyard, it was the Lunar cats' attempts to stop her that drew attention from the locals and got the story into the papers – in particular, people kept spotting the enormous (but rather stupid) cat known as Mr Bruise. Most of the Lunar cats have made nice homes with families in the vicinity; they rarely meet as a society; but all of them responded to the call for action when it came. Although they don't know the full story of the Oviri yet, they know that its arrival in the summer of 1771 coincided with the death of their learned friend Hodge, and precipitated the end of their dear, hubristic Cat Master, Hawkesworth; they also suspect it ruined for ever the life of their friend Thomas Timkins, who had sailed on the *Endeavour*. Plus, of course, it's just a terrifying object in itself. They are distraught that it has now been successfully excavated by a demon kitten who sounds like Barbara Windsor and her ghastly female minion who smells of casserole reheated in a vestry. To be frank, the Lunar cats will be useless in a battle against Tetty, being more interested in the complex muscular arrangement of the feline ear – but they have goodness and numbers on their side. They have also waited nearly two hundred and fifty years for something to happen, so it would be criminal not to include them in our plans.'

Roger looked pleased with himself. He loved being in this position, of knowing everything, and parcelling out information on a need-to-know basis which he himself determined.

'Roger?' I said.

He smiled at me. 'I'm so sorry about the mouthey-mouthey, Alec. I think you're now stuck with it, but if you cover it with a piece of card, at least it won't randomly suck up tissues and peanuts and fluff and so on.'

I was glad of the tip. 'Thank you, Roger. But what I wanted to ask was: you mentioned the cat Timkins.'

Roger swallowed and gave us a brave and knowing smile. 'Yes,' he said, softly. 'This is all about Timkins, really. All of it.'

Wiggy was completely lost. 'It's all about *who*?'

I realised this wasn't fair on Wiggy, but I felt I should press on. I could always explain it all later.

'Am I right in thinking that the Thomas Timkins who sailed to Tahiti later went by the name of "the Captain"?'

* * *

When we met at six thirty, Wiggy remembered to put the 'Do Not Disturb' sign on the doorknob outside – which was an excellent thought, when you consider how difficult it would be to explain to a startled chambermaid the presence in my hotel room of a dozen assorted cats, all of them with the power of speech, some of them wearing wigs and taking snuff and sneezing. They arrived as a group, getting slightly wedged in the doorway; then they separated, a bit ruffled, and introduced themselves. As they entered the room, I felt a strange tugging sensation in my ankle, which I resisted. On Roger's advice, I had taped something over the mouthey-mouthey. A postcard had turned out to be too inflexible for the job, so in the end I'd used an old muslin lavender bag I found in a chest of drawers, fixing it to my hairy leg by means of sticky tape. Wiggy, using his good left hand (the other being useless), helped me with the fixing. He agreed with my own impression that the mouthey-mouthey fought back throughout the entire operation, and emitted a sort of muffled snarling noise at the end of it.

Roger made sure that everyone was comfortable before beginning. He was aware that some of us knew more of Timkins's story than others. Before commencing, therefore, he asked the Lunar cats to stop him whenever he deviated from their own remembered version of events. (This was big of him; he obviously held the Lunar cats in high regard.) He also explained that Wiggy and I had both been injured by the Oviri, and had been present at the eventual demise of Timkins, but he didn't go into details, for fear they would either streak off in terror when they saw the mouthey-mouthey, or attack me and kill me with their own claws when they heard how I had, deliberately, on that snowy night at Harville, run over the Captain twice in my tank-like Volvo.

'In 1768,' Roger began, 'young Thomas Timkins boarded the *Endeavour* at Deptford, where the ship was provisioning. He was two years old, of splendid upbringing, with an excellent mind. In short, a gentle and intellectually curious member of the illustrious London Lunar Society, as are all of you to this day.'

There was a murmur of gracious miaows at this, and a bit of purring; a smattering of applause. Some of the Lunar cats shot a glance at a large ginger tom (who turned out to be Mr MacJockie), but at this stage Wiggy and I had no idea why they would want to exempt him from the general description of 'gentle'. One of the other cats, however, nodded his head so firmly that his wig fell off.

'One day we will recover the *Endeavour* journal of young Thomas Timkins,' Roger continued, 'and we will see precisely what happened to him on this three-year voyage to the South Seas. What I know for certain is that many of his expectations were cruelly dashed. He had hoped for enlightening discussions with Mr Banks and Dr Solander, two followers of the great classifier Linnaeus; he had hoped to share navigational duties with the peerless James Cook! But throughout the voyage he had little contact with the residents of the Great Cabin; within a couple of months at sea he was unjustly accused of killing a pet bird, which ruined any chance of his falling into favour with Mr Banks. Plus there were some incredibly annoying dogs on board. For a young intellectual cat, burning with scientific curiosity, being mere yards away from empirical revolutions in botany and zoology; being yards from the greatest map-making the world had ever seen; being yards from the best botanical drawing and the best astronomy – to be shut out of these activities for *three whole years* was not just disappointing; it was crushing.'

Roger paused. He had noticed that the Lunar cats were all whispering amongst themselves. They stopped when they realised he was looking at them.

'Is it the voice?' he asked when they were quiet. 'Are you trying to decide who my voice sounds like?'

It was not aggressive, but they were discomfited none the less. He had evidently hit the mark.

'Well, yes,' admitted Mr Nolly (a slender black cat with a sensitive face). 'I'm afraid to say it is a little distracting trying to think who you—'

I intervened. I couldn't help it. 'Vincent Price!' I said.

'Ahhhh! Mmmmm.'

A great sigh of relief went up, and they visibly relaxed. I knew the feeling. But how interesting that these elevated, deathless Lunar cats had evidently spent the 1960s watching terrible Roger Corman films, just like all the rest of us.

Roger resumed. 'Timkins had been encouraged to undertake the expedition by the chosen Cat Master of the day, Dr John Hawkesworth.'

The cats all miaowed in approving chorus at the sound of their mentor's name.

Roger took a deep breath. 'What I have to tell you today is that to the end of his life, Timkins was deeply pained by any memory of Dr Hawkesworth.'

The cats narrowed their eyes, and I noticed that a few claws were instinctively flexed.

'Like you all,' Roger said, 'Timkins had adored his Cat Master. Like you all, he had thought the Cat Master's entire concern was the happiness and well-being of you special, clever Lunar cats. But Timkins's experiences regarding the voyage and its aftermath taught him to see a different side of your "good doctor". As I shall explain.'

As Roger began again with the story, I found myself transported to the small wooden Whitby cat that Captain Cook had commanded. I heard the creaking timbers and the crack of wind in the sails; the ringing of the bell (*ding-ding, ding-ding*); the men heaving on the ropes. Beyond the dense, swinging rigging of the ship, I could see nothing but sea and sky, and I even felt a wave of navigational panic: *How do we know where we are, or what direction we're sailing in?* And all the time, I felt the deck dipping side to side, and I found that, before long, I was physically rocking back and forth in my chair – and when I looked around the room, I saw that

Roger's words had affected everyone in the same way: all of us were gently rocking, rocking, as if we were at sea.

'Life as a sailor was a surprise to young Timkins,' said Roger. 'At first he fell ill; he was also horrified by the noise and the smells and the people. Ninety-four men were aboard that hundred-foot ship – eating, sleeping, farting, snoring, drinking, washing, defecating. He had never appreciated the skill involved in keeping a ship moving; keeping it heading in the right direction; keeping the men healthy and fed; keeping the ship clean. Dr Hawkesworth had lied to him about the length of the voyage, I'm afraid—'

The cats reacted, but didn't interrupt.

'He had told Timkins he would be home by September. In fact, the voyage was always anticipated to last at least a couple of years. Captain Cook carried sealed instructions. When the astronomical observations had been completed in Tahiti, he was to sail south, and search for the Great Southern Continent – which at the time was undiscovered, although many men of science believed it to be there.'

'And women,' piped up a small voice from the cats. 'Men and women of science.' We all looked round.

It was Mrs Stella. I had noticed that she usually appeared in smaller print than the others, and it was interesting that she actually *sounded* like someone in smaller print.

Roger nodded an acknowledgement to the only female present, and then continued, 'The point is that the voyage thereby grew to three years. Timkins was soon extremely homesick. He kept his journal faithfully; he drew charts; he kept company with the ship's surgeon, Mr Monkhouse, to whom he had revealed his powers of speech and reason. And all the time he wondered why his dear Dr Hawkesworth had really sent him on the voyage. He remembered a troubling conversation he had had with Mr Hodge, and I suppose I should ask you: were you aware that Mr Hodge, may he rest in peace, was somewhat critical of Dr Hawkesworth?'

'Oh yes,' they said, shaking their heads in sorrow.

The black cat (Nolly) explained, 'It was difficult for him. Mr Hodge was a genius. The cleverest of us by far.'

The others joined in:

'He wrote sophisticated comedies for David Garrick!'

'He gave Voltaire the idea for *Candide*!'

'He invented a primitive calculating machine!'

'It was his fault King George went mad! Hodge spoke German more beautifully than he did!'

Nolly acknowledged all this, and continued, 'But he was loyal to Dr Johnson, who was never very rich; it was difficult for him that our dear Cat Master met with so many plaudits, honours and material rewards.'

'Thank you,' said Roger. 'On the ship, you see, Timkins found that a conversation with Mr Hodge kept tugging at his memory. Mr Hodge had said that a "smell of sulphur" hung over the post of Cat Master. He also warned Timkins that Dr Hawkesworth was ruthlessly ambitious and exploited his friends. Haunted by this conversation, Timkins recorded it in his journal. He later had every reason to wish he had not set it down.'

As Roger was talking, I got quite emotional. Timkins's loneliness at sea; his wasted talent; and now his sense that he might be betrayed by the very man he was devoted to – I felt it all. I not only rocked back and forward and heard the *ding-dings*; I felt a great aching sorrow for this small, trusting being who had started out with such hope in his heart; who had later created Roger as an ETC; and who had ended up (the bastard) scaring me and my blameless little dog half to death in Dorset, battering the snowy windscreen of our car like a veritable cat out of hell.

'As the ship made its way south in the Atlantic, Timkins grew to be a better sailor. He allowed himself to be thought of as the surgeon's cat, and he cautiously befriended those on board whose prejudice against cats was of the least. Although others went ashore at the stopping points – Madeira, Tierra del Fuego – Timkins remained aboard. When he had embarked on this voyage he had been a fearless character, but the realities of ship life soon wore him down, and it didn't help that the surgeon, Mr Monkhouse, treated all such disorders of the soul with undiluted alcohol. By the time Timkins returned to London in 1771, as you know, he was a very different cat. But the fact that he hadn't gone insane is very much to his credit.

'We know that Captain Cook had sealed orders. Timkins had sealed orders, too. He had been instructed (by Hawkesworth) not to open these orders until the ship had reached Tahiti. But sometime in the spring of 1769, while the ship was heading north-west from the Cape of Good

Hope, Timkins decided to retrieve his orders from where he had hidden them in the Great Cabin. And he found, to his great dismay, that they *were not there.* It was a terrible moment for him. He had been entrusted with some secret mission by Dr Hawkesworth, and now he didn't know what it was! And it could have been anything! He might have been commissioned to measure the island, calculate its weight, describe its fauna, notate its language, classify its trees, log its longitude – anything! And now his sealed instructions had gone missing; the entire purpose of his presence on the voyage was cancelled, and he simply broke down. One hundred and fifty years after these events – as he and I sat on the deck of a small fishing vessel off the coast of Albania, in the 1930s, under a star-filled sky – he described this desolated feeling to me. He had not realised until that point that Dr Hawkesworth's trust in him had sustained him through so much. He had seen himself as an Intrepid Lunar Cat. But now that he was an Intrepid Lunar Cat Without Portfolio, he was utterly destroyed.'

A voice piped up. It was a thin yellow cat called Mr Tinkle. He asked if he could be briefly excused.

Roger said yes, and promised not to continue until he came back.

It was like coming out of a trance. I stopped rocking in my chair. I remembered my ankle. I cleared my throat and, in a general sort of way, addressed the Lunar cats. 'Poor Timkins. Did he tell you all of this when he returned?'

'Very little of it,' said Nolly, who was emerging as the most communicative of the group. 'But I feel sure, sir, that Thomas Timkins had more resources than Mr Roger suggests. Leaving aside the instructions, he was a cat of science, and this voyage would present him with many paths of enquiry and investigation of his own. The loss of the paper need not have deprived him of all purpose.'

'Well, it did,' said Roger, flatly.

There was an awkward pause, during which Mr Tinkle returned, whispering, 'Thank you'; and Roger returned to the story.

'To continue,' he said. 'You all know of the Oviri.'

It was a shock tactic. The animals all hissed at its name, and some of them instinctively cowered.

'You know that it returned with Timkins in 1771.'

'It followed him!' cried Nolly. 'It followed him off the boat and all the way to Bromley. It wasn't his fault!'

Roger's expression gave nothing away.

'On the thirteenth of April 1769, the *Endeavour* reached Matavai Bay in Tahiti. It is important to remember that Cook did not discover Tahiti – far from it. Previous European ships had been there; the Admiralty and the Royal Society in London had chosen Tahiti as a known place from which to observe the transit of Venus in June. However, contact between the Tahitians and visitors had been more limited on previous occasions. The *Endeavour* stayed three months in total, mostly quite peaceably. As was written up by Dr Hawkesworth in his account of the voyage, at Tahiti there were regrettable scuffles with the natives; also a good deal of botanising, and an incredible amount of sex.

'Timkins was only once taken ashore. The surgeon's opinion was that the longest possible lifespan of a small European cat on shore in Tahiti would be about two and a half minutes. But Timkins's frustration was so intense that on one occasion Monkhouse carried him ashore on his back, in a papoose of rough sailcloth, and carried him half a mile or so inland to see a *marae* – or sacred altar. Timkins said that the heat and flies were horrible; that the smell of dense vegetation nearly choked him; and that the celebrated lascivious womenfolk left him cold; but to see such primitive religious productions was quite inspiring. That evening, for the first time in months, his journal was lively and full of philosophy.

'The sojourn on Tahiti did change things on the ship for him. The Great Cabin was now not constantly in use by Banks and Solander, or (more importantly) the dogs. Timkins would visit Mr Parkinson, the artist, and watch him at work, making his astonishing drawings and watercolours, and battling with the legions of flies who ate the colour from the paper as soon as it was laid. Over the months, Mr Parkinson and a few others in the crew had become vaguely aware of Timkins's power of speech (it helped that everyone was drunk most of the time). Now, as the ship was moored in Matavai Bay, Timkins increased his friendships with several of the crew: with a gunner's servant called Daniel Roberts, and with Mr Monkhouse's brother Jonathan, a midshipman. Also one of the privates of the marines called Preston; also the ship's butcher, Henry Jeffs. By the time the voyage recommenced, Timkins had half a dozen friends, all committed to helping him through the long, long voyage ahead.

'Naturally, he revelled in all the findings at Tahiti. Mr Parkinson would show him the specimens, and report to him on the great advances he was personally making in understanding the natives. Mr Parkinson compiled a glossary of Tahitian words, and he tried to use them. In fact, between Parkinson and Timkins, it became a sort of secret language; so that, for example, he used to whisper to Timkins, "*Mamoo!*" – meaning "Hold your tongue" – when he thought there was a danger of his being overheard. He said to Timkins once that, actually, the Tahitian language might have been invented by cats, there were so many "iaow" sounds in it. The word for "myself" was *naow*; "speak to me" was *paraow mai*; "it stinks" was *whaow whaow*.'

The Lunar cats laughed at this, and one of them made a note.

'And one day, Mr Parkinson returned to the ship with a small, carved, wooden idol, that he called *Oviri-moe-ahere* ("the savage who sleeps in the forest"), and explained to Timkins that it represented the Tahitian goddess of death and mourning. He placed it on his desk. It was a female figure, nine inches tall, embodying violent, howling grief – eyes large and accusing; mouth dropped open in bottomless misery; hair in wild disarray. Parkinson seemed particularly pleased with it. Timkins asked him why he would take such a thing. And at this point, Parkinson produced from where it was tucked inside his journal a sheet of paper on which Timkins recognised at once, with some confusion, the orthography of Dr John Hawkesworth.'

Wiggy fidgeted.

'Handwriting,' I whispered.

'Cheers,' he whispered back.

'Parkinson spread the paper for Timkins to see,' said Roger. '"This was sealed up, Timkins, with no name on," he said. "It says that to transport the *Oviri-moe-ahere* to London will be of the highest possible value to men of science working there. It will bring lasting fame and fortune to him who brings it. I am to hide it away, and on my return to London, to take it directly to the office of the *Gentleman's Magazine* in St John's Gate, Clerkenwell, to claim my reward!"

'Timkins was very confused. Hawkesworth had sent him all this way to steal a religious artefact? To *steal*? To steal for *money and fame*? "Does it say anything about counting grains of sand, or calculating barometric pressure, or observing planets in retrograde?" he asked. Parkinson shook his head. "No, it just says, locate the idol, seize the idol, share with no one knowledge of the idol – so I've slipped up there, but *mamoo*'s the word, young Timkins – then it says put it in a box and keep it secure until you return to England. Oh, and there's a note at the bottom, saying, 'Don't overthink this, young fellow, I know what you're like.' I do wonder whether I was the intended recipient of these instructions, but no one has ever come looking for them, and they were put in the cupboard where I keep my paints!"

'For Timkins the rest of the voyage was torture. All he wanted was to get back to England to uncover Hawkesworth's purpose in sending him to procure this evil-looking object. After Tahiti, the ship spent months circling New Zealand, while the captain drew detailed maps of unprecedented accuracy. Timkins didn't care. He was drinking (or lapping) heavily. After New Zealand, they travelled up the east coast of Australia – or New Holland, as they called it then. Timkins hardly got out of bed. He kept his journal throughout, but there was nothing about wind speed or nautical business: just his increasingly unhappy nostalgia for the world of innocence he had left behind. When the ship foundered on the coral reef off the coast of Queensland and nearly sank, Timkins roused himself briefly to consider how he might save himself and his writings, but when the danger was over, he resumed his former moods. Monkhouse, finally realising that gin might be at the root of the trouble, attempted to reform Timkins's drinking habits, but it was too late. "*Mamoo,*" Timkins would say to him, and then giggle. As the ship approached Batavia (modern-day Jakarta), Monkhouse organised an intervention by all Timkins's friends on board: Jonathan Monkhouse, Mr Parkinson, the butcher, the gunner's lad and so on. But it did no good. Monkhouse felt terrible. Timkins was lapping himself into an early grave.

'And then, at Batavia, in November 1770, the unthinkable happened. Mr Monkhouse died. This was a great blow for Timkins. It seems that water taken aboard at Batavia was contaminated;

Mr Monkhouse was immediately replaced by his deputy, who saw no reason to cohabit with Monkhouse's miserable, lazy, drunken cat. So, as well as losing his greatest friend, Timkins lost his cosy nest, and was also cut off from his alcohol supply. Mr Parkinson offered to smuggle Timkins into his own quarters, but Timkins was wary of the influence of the idol, and said so. Parkinson laughed it off as superstition, saying Timkins had definitely become a proper sailor if he let himself believe in the "influence" of a wooden doll! And then he admitted that sometimes he thought the doll did rattle in its box; and that once, when handling it, he had received a puncture to his wrist that had become so oddly infected that he dared not show it to anyone. Also, that he had once discovered the idol outside of its box, which circumstance he could not adequately explain.

'Seven men in all were to die at Batavia. Timkins was as upset as everyone else. Cook's insistence on a regime of hygiene and fresh food (and sauerkraut) had, up to now, kept nearly everyone alive. And now an epidemic had visited the ship, and as it sailed south-west across the Indian Ocean, Timkins was aware of two things; and his journal became full of them. That at night there was frequently a fast scuttling, knocking noise along the decks; and that by day men were found either with parts of themselves roughly bandaged (first), or afterwards dead, often with their surroundings in strange disarray, as if they had lashed and writhed in their death throes. On the night of the twenty-fifth of January 1771 – after three deaths in short succession – Timkins decided to visit Parkinson, to advance his theory that the Oviri was to blame for this plague, and to beg him to cast it overboard. But as he entered Parkinson's quarters, he saw in the darkness a scene that would haunt him for ever: Parkinson was asleep in his hammock but moaning, and around him all the movable objects in the small cabin had lifted into the air and were circling his body. Parkinson was muttering Tahitian words, in a kind of trance. A slow but powerful vortex was building up in the room, and Timkins had to hold fast to the door frame to save himself from being sucked into it. And then the idol slithered into the room – "slither" was the word he used – and launched itself towards Parkinson. When Parkinson started to scream, Timkins ran away. As a friend, he should have tried to help; as a scientist, he knew he should have observed and made notes. But as a cat, all his instincts told him to turn tail and run away as if his little furry bottom was on fire.

'Within a month, all of Timkins's friends were dead. One by one, the gunner's servant, the butcher, Jonathan Monkhouse – all of them. The whole of the rest of the voyage – another six long months – he spent hunting the idol, trying to trap the idol; considering how to destroy it; telling himself over and over that Hawkesworth could not possibly know how dangerous it was. When he finally disembarked in England, he took a coach here to Bromley, but did not instantly return to the Grete House. For one thing, he knew it would be a couple of weeks before he could walk properly, but mainly he was afraid that the idol might follow him. So, first storing his journals at this very inn, he slept rough in London. One night, in fact, he spied on you all, at your favourite Wig and Gavel tavern—'

'No!' The Lunar cats were pained to hear it.

'Yes. He said he heard you all solemnly discussing a paper on the electrical-conducting properties of the cat's whisker—'

'That was mine!' said Mrs Stella.

'And he wept to hear you. Such gentle tones; such intellectual airiness. He told me later that the idea of cats conducting electricity between themselves via their whiskers was so brilliant that he could barely contain himself from shouting "Brava, Mrs Stella" – but he knew he could never come back fully to your company, his sense of failure as a would-be navigator being so immense. Eventually, he crawled home to Dr Hawkesworth's house, arranging for his journals to be left for the dear doctor to see, and collapsed. He was nursed by Mrs Hawkesworth for the next few months, and when he had finally recovered, there was big news waiting for him. Dr Hawkesworth had hit the literary jackpot of the age! He had been commissioned by the Admiralty – based on no nautical expertise whatsoever – to write up the very voyage to the South Seas that Timkins had experienced, and was to receive six thousand pounds, an unthinkable sum! With the money, he would be able to purchase the Grete House (which until then he had merely rented); he would also be able to dedicate his book to the King, and become an investor in the great East India Company! Previously, Hawkesworth had been suspiciously successful, given the extent of his talents. But now, since Timkins's return, he was a made man. Six thousand pounds! And all the while, it seems that no one – or *no one apart from Hodge* – guessed the obvious truth: that he was getting unfair help from supernatural forces.'

The Lunar cats coughed and fidgeted.

'We will pause in a moment,' said Roger. 'I know there is a lot here for you cats to take in. You thought Dr Hawkesworth sent Timkins on the voyage to broaden his mind.'

A murmur of sad affirmative miaows, with sniffs.

'Whereas in fact Dr Hawkesworth was so incredibly ambitious, and so full of hubris, that he hoped, with the aid of this truly evil exotic artefact, to break even with his employer Satan and – as it were – go into competition with him.'

There was a general gasp. Mr Tinkle asked to be excused again. To everyone's surprise, Roger refused, saying he had nearly finished with the first part of the story. He reminded us, quickly, that Timkins had just recovered from his illness, and had heard about the £6,000. Hawkesworth had seemed pleased to see him well again, although he'd clearly had hurtful reservations about how badly Timkins had accomplished his three years before the mast. And he started with the worst possible information.

'"My boy," he said to Timkins, "you will grieve to hear this, but I fear that your journals, to which you so tirelessly committed yourself for over a thousand days at sea, suffered badly from water damage and were therefore useless to me."

'Timkins froze in shock and disbelief. He had seen the journals himself since arriving on dry land, and there had been nothing wrong with them. He was uncertain how to react. For the present, all he could manage, with a dry mouth, was the word "Really?"

'Hawkesworth patted him on the head. "I am so sorry, Timkins. To save you the distress of seeing them in their ruined state, I immediately ordered their destruction."

'Timkins swallowed hard.

'"But despite all your myriad failures on the *Endeavour*, my boy, I am not ungrateful to you; you doubtless did your best. And I can offer consolation: you will assist me in writing my three-volume account of the South Sea voyages, and receive a share of the credit!"

'Timkins said nothing. He had hoped to put the voyage behind him, and return to softer pursuits. He had been dreaming, throughout his feverish convalescence, of starting a brewery in Southwark. Could he bear to re-live the voyage, even in literary form? He now realised that on Hawkesworth's desk were stacked a number of large volumes that he recognised from the Great Cabin – the journals of Cook and Banks and Parkinson. It felt strange to see them there.

'He made a decision. "Can you tell me, sir," he asked quietly, "what says the peerless Lieutenant Cook for the day of the fifth of November 1770?"

'Hawkesworth proudly produced the relevant volume and turned to the page. He showed it to Timkins. On the fifth, the entry was lacking what he sought; in the entry two days later, Timkins found the following:

> "'*Wednesday seventh.* Employ'd getting ready to heave down. In the PM we had the missfortune to loose Mr Monkhouse the Surgeon who died at Batavia after a short illness of which disease and others, several of our people are

daly taken ill which make his loss be the more severly felt. He was succeeded by Mr Perry his mate, who is equally well if not better skilld in his profession."

'Remembering what he himself had written in tribute to Mr Monkhouse, in the journal that was lost, Timkins staggered in his misery. But as he did so, he was aware of the expressions that competed on Dr Hawkesworth's face – and they confirmed his worst suspicions. A fleeting malicious smile gave way to a frown of concern, and then the smile reasserted itself broadly when, unmistakably, a familiar rattling, knocking noise came from inside Dr Hawkesworth's desk, and Timkins stifled a scream.

'"Ah, yes," said his dear doctor. "There is yet more good fortune to report. Although you arrived home without it, which I will confess caused me sore disappointment, dear Timkins, my Tahitian prize was but a little way behind you! You cannot conceive my delight in receiving it! It knocked on my window some two months ago and since then has been safe and sound in the drawer of my desk!"'

Chapter Five

Someone switched the lights on. I think it was me. The Lunar cats, while remarkable in so many ways, were still incapable (on account of their normal cat stature) of reaching halfway up a wall. As we all struggled to emerge from our narrative trance, Roger suggested we take a break of fifteen minutes, and for the sake of Mr Tinkle I opened the door and he streaked out, while the others wordlessly jumped down to the floor from their various chairs and surfaces, and huddled together, making murmurs and faint miaows, all indicative of having been greatly disturbed by poor Timkins's story. Wiggy was looking a bit green. Roger's dismal description of the Oviri's disgusting activities while aboard the *Endeavour* had left us in no doubt what we were up against. To think I had been within just a few feet of this malevolent object! I had already been primed for a fatal attack! I looked around and recognised the truth of my situation: as things currently stood, my only defences against a horrific Polynesian-derived death with stuff flying around the room were these:

1. Roger (a cat)
2. a bunch of terrified and intellectual cats from the eighteenth century
3. a well-meaning idiot, and
4. a loosely taped-on lavender bag.

Roger asked if I was all right. I said I'd like to go outside and check my phone – which I didn't really care about; I just needed not to talk to Roger until the Timkins story was finished. I asked Wiggy if he wanted to join me in a little stroll, but he said no. He was still seated, nursing his injured hand, and looking unusually thoughtful. I felt a pang at the sight of this – to see Wiggy so concerned on my behalf.

'I'll be all right,' I said quietly.

He looked up and smiled. 'Sorry?'

'I was just saying not to worry about me.'

'Oh.'

'Roger's probably got a brilliant plan. And I bet the conductivity of the cat's whisker will come into it somehow. The Lunar cats will somehow make a circuit with their whiskers and electrocute the Oviri, or they'll . . .'

He looked at me with such a pained expression that I faltered and stopped. It was true that I was talking nonsense. The Lunar cats were less a secret weapon in all this, more a bizarre encumbrance.

Outside it was raining, so I trotted to the car park and got into the trusty Volvo. Shivering, I switched on the heater, locked the doors and shut my eyes for a minute or two. Then, just because I had used the phone as my excuse, I retrieved it from my back pocket and turned it on – and it was there, in the rainy dark, that I discovered four missed calls, three of them from the vet's in Cambridge where Watson was safely spending his extortionate convalescence. The vet's calls had been made at 6.40, 6.48 and 6.55. The other call, from a number I didn't recognise, had been made at 8 p.m.

'Mr Charlesworth, could you call the St Francis Veterinary Surgery, please? Something's happened. There'll be someone here till seven. It's quite urgent.'

This was the unnerving 6.40 message. I played the next one. It was a different voice. The first had been the receptionist. The new one was the vet herself.

'Hello, Alec?' She sounded tense. 'Alec, please call when you get this. It's Watson. I don't know how it happened! I'll try you again this evening from home, but this is just to say I'm so sorry, desperately sorry, and please call.'

I played the third message.

'Alec, the surgery is closing now. I'll call from home later. Basically what's happened is, Watson's gone. We've been trying to work out how someone managed to unlock the back door, and we think it was when an old lady brought this tiny beautiful ginger kitten in this afternoon, because she went off to use the loo and we all got distracted by this little ginger kitten because it was so lovely and I'm so sorry, Alec, you'll be worried, and you'll be angry with us, but who would do such a thing, plot to take an ordinary little dog from a vet's? And to be fair, you should have seen this kitten!'

I was just about to play the last message when there was a knock at the window. I jumped in the air. It was Wiggy. I unlocked the doors and he quickly got in.

'Sorry about just now,' he said.

'That's OK.'

'I was just thinking how I'm always an early victim!'

I laughed. He laughed too – but I had a feeling he wasn't joking.

'Greater impact!' I said.

'That's right. That's right.'

We sat in silence for a moment. I was in an agony of concern about Watson, desperate to listen to the fourth message, but I knew I mustn't say anything yet.

'Any messages?' he said.

'What?'

'Your phone.'

'Oh. No.'

It wasn't that I wanted to lie to Wiggy, but my mind was racing and I knew that if I told him all I knew, he would ask follow-up questions (Where did they take him? Why did they take him? Do you think he's alive?), which would drive me mad for a mixture of reasons. Also, in kidnap situations, isn't it always the first rule: don't tell anyone?

Wiggy sat in silence for a while (which is not like him), and drew breath to say something – but decided against it. In any other situation, I would have encouraged him to say what was on his mind. But right now, I was glad not to be distracted any further from the enormous news I was struggling to absorb.

'Do you think Tetty really did mastermind that raid in Hatton Garden?' Wiggy said at last (presumably instead of the other thing).

'I have no doubt whatsoever,' I said.

He laughed and opened the door. 'Are you coming?'

'In a minute,' I said.

It was then, when Wiggy was darting away into the rainy darkness, that I listened to the final message. It was not from the vet to say they had found Watson in a cupboard and it had all been a regrettable false alarm. It was, of course, from Tetty.

Back inside, Roger resumed his story a few minutes later, when his audience had reassembled. He was slightly impatient with me for being the last to arrive, but I was determined to make no explanation or apology. Watson had been kidnapped, and I had been given strict instructions to follow. Tetty evidently found the whole thing highly amusing. 'All those bleeding films with surprise endings you made me watch, trying to get me to say "*Oo-er*"!' she'd laughed. Playful but hard; feminine but rasping; coy but with an edge of threat – yes, I'd been right about the voice: the similarity to Barbara Windsor was remarkable. If Tetty had not opted for a criminal career, a life of saucy voice-overs might well have been hers. 'Well, here's a real *oo-er* for you, treacle. I got your precious doggie.' In the background, I had been able to hear a woman calling, 'Teatime, Kitty-cat!' At which Tetty had turned from the phone and shouted, 'Oh, zip it, grandma, for Christ's sake.' And then there had been a faint disgruntled woof, which I knew to be Watson. Then Tetty had laughed again and told me what to do, and then she'd said, 'All right, then. Toodle-oo.' And then she was gone.

Knowing none of this, Roger was, as I said, impatient with my late arrival, but he grew even more cross with me as he recommenced his story, because – and this was understandable in the circumstances – I was no longer happy with his slow-burning, tension-building approach to narrative. For one thing, we'd already had two hours of it, and were feeling seasick. For another, I now had an urgent meeting elsewhere in Bromley at half past nine.

'We left our story with Hawkesworth receiving the commission to write the *Voyages*,' he said. 'He was on top of the world. Feted, rich, illustrious. But by the end of 1773 he was utterly destroyed.'

The Lunar cats looked doleful at the bitter memory of it all. They settled down for another long session, lying in relaxed positions. I even heard some inappropriate purring from Mr Tinkle (he received a sharp nudge in the ribs, and desisted).

'How could this have happened?' Roger asked, rhetorically.

A bit of sniffing from the Lunar cats.

'How,' Roger continued, 'could a man with such success, money, influence and respect – and such firm support from supernatural quarters, don't forget – end up not only a victim of hostile criticism, but dead? And not only dead, but completely forgotten thereafter, as if by historical conspiracy?'

I put my hand up. Roger gave me a look – a look that said, unequivocally, *Don't even think about it.*

However, I ignored the look. I kept my hand raised. 'Ooh! Ooh!' I said. 'I know! I know!'

Wiggy laughed at the nerve of it. Some of the Lunar cats tittered.

Roger drew breath. But he didn't get very far. 'What we must remember is that the Admiralty in this period—'

'Ooh! I know!' I said again. 'Roger, may I?'

'Alec, what is it?'

'It's just that I've got a theory, Roger. May I?' And before Roger could stop me, I ploughed on. 'Of course, Hawkesworth had read Timkins's journal,' I said. 'I mean, I bet he was lying when he said it had been damaged.'

I looked round. The others seemed happy for me to continue. They settled down even more comfortably in their chairs.

'He had two reasons for telling Timkins it was unreadable. First, he didn't want Timkins to think he'd played any useful role in Hawkesworth getting the commission – which I expect he had. Second, because of the passage about Hodge.'

A collective shudder of gasps and 'Oh no!'s wiffled through the cats.

'Hawkesworth was furious with Hodge after reading what Timkins wrote. As a man who cared deeply about his future literary reputation, he now knew for certain that Hodge was a threat. He therefore resolved to deal with him. Am I right so far?'

Roger looked very angry. His tail was swishing from side to side. 'Alec,' he said. 'I'd much rather you didn't jump ahead like this. It will confuse everyone.'

'Am I right, though?' I said.

'It sounds very plausible to me,' said Wiggy.

'Am I right, though?' I repeated.

The others were keen to know this too. They demanded to know it. Is Alec right? Is he right? Is he? Is he? Is he?

There was a long pause while Roger decided how to react. 'Well, yes,' he conceded at last. 'Broadly. Alec is broadly right.'

This bad grace on his part did not go down well. The others said 'Tsk' at him. It must have been insufferable for Roger to have his position of authority undercut like this, but I had far too much on my mind to care about his injured feelings.

'But there's a lot more to it!' he insisted. 'Please, Alec. This is all too *broad*.'

I didn't really care about the breadth. It was the length that I was worried about, which is why I pressed on.

'But when Hawkesworth disposed of the brilliant Hodge – no doubt deploying the Oviri . . . ?'

I looked pointedly at Roger for confirmation. Then everyone else looked pointedly at him too. In the end, Roger grudgingly nodded his assent.

'As I say, when he used the Oviri on Hodge, Hawkesworth finally overreached himself, and sealed his own fate. His diabolical line manager, who would have been, I don't know, Beelzebub or whatever . . . ?'

I paused. By now he knew the drill. 'Beelzebub, yes,' Roger said sulkily.

'Well, Beelzebub was enraged. How dare this talentless Hawkesworth contend with the Supreme Evil Being? And then there was probably a fantastic, scary showdown between Hawkesworth and the Devil that Timkins observed . . . ?'

'Yes.' Roger was looking like thunder.

'And then Hawkesworth overnight lost everything. Everything. All his standing, his power, his indefinable *luck*. Even though the *Voyages* are actually *really good*' – I felt I had to say this – 'he got terrible, vicious reviews. Everyone turned on him. The public declared the *Voyages* to be irreligious, lewd, or just wrong. He was stripped of his Cat Master status. This is why, in the pamphlet *Nine Lives*, his real name isn't even listed. It just says "The Adventurer". All that Beelzebub had granted him, Beelzebub simply took away. Hawkesworth became a mere man again, a forgotten man, and would still be forgotten if he hadn't been buried – no doubt at poor Timkins's absolute insistence – with the Oviri beside him, which Tetty the kitten has now dug up and is intending to use!'

And there I stopped, expecting to be in trouble for ruining such a good story. But in fact – much to the annoyance of Roger – I got an enthusiastic round of applause.

'Bravo!' said Signor Andreotti.

'Well done,' said Mr Nolly.

'You have a fine deductive mind!' exclaimed Mrs Stella, 'and I salute you!'

I looked at Roger. Would he forgive me? Well, the first signs were good: he graciously offered a paw. As I shook it (what a gentleman he is!), he said quietly, 'I need to know why you did this, Alec.'

But I shrugged as if there were no reason, and then I calmed the applause and said, 'I'm sure my account left many questions unanswered, and that Roger can fill them in. But in the meantime, if you will excuse me? Sorry, Wiggy, can't explain!' And I left the room. It was like a stage exit, I realised afterwards. A bit am-dram. But at least I hadn't first removed a revolver from a desk drawer. And it was effective, too. They were all so puzzled by the theatricality (and wondering what play it reminded them of) that they didn't follow me. In a couple of minutes I was in the car; a few minutes more and I was outside the church, in the gusty rain, waiting for a woman who smelled of stew to take me to my own personal showdown with a ruthless, diabolical criminal genius in the shape of a gorgeous kitten.

I had forgotten how very gorgeous Tetty was. When we entered the small terraced house where she and Mrs Fletcher were waiting for me, my first impulse was to run to the sofa – where she was lying stretched out on her back, with all four paws in the air – and pick her up and nuzzle her (fortunately I overcame this impulse). It was Mrs Fletcher's older sister who had collected me from the church. Under orders not to tell me anything, she only said (out of fairness, I think) that the vicar had called the police directly after seeing me and Wiggy cavorting outside the church in the morning, and that they might still be looking for us. Interestingly, her other instructions did not include blindfolding me, or in any way disorientating me so that I would not find the address again. Tetty was so confident, I suppose, that her hold over me (dear Watson) was secure enough to make me do anything she wanted.

Tetty sat up when she saw me. She yawned, showing her tiny sharp teeth.

'Well, here's Alec bleeding Charlesworth,' she said, 'or I'm not Davy Crockett, King of the Wild Frontier. How's the leg?'

'Hello, Tetty,' I said steadily. The Davy Crockett reference rang faint bells from childhood, but I refused to waste time establishing what she was talking about. As for the leg, I thought it sensible to ignore the question. As a matter of fact, it had started throbbing and twitching the moment we'd entered the house.

Mrs Fletcher came in from the kitchen, carrying with difficulty a heavy golden cat bowl with glistening black fish eggs in it.

'Kitty dear,' she said. 'Your favourite!'

But she was waved away. 'Not now, for Gawd's sake!' Tetty barked.

Stung, Mrs Fletcher retreated. And I have to say, I felt sorry for her. It is no fate for anyone, being the slave of a cat (as millions of ordinary cat owners can attest); but to be the *actual* slave of an *evil talking kitten with Napoleonic ambitions* is exceptionally tough, in my view. As Mrs Fletcher backed away and then turned to leave the room, I realised I'd never looked at her face before. To my surprise, she wasn't particularly old. She was perhaps in her late forties. Maybe she had been widowed or divorced, had innocently visited a cat rescue centre in hope of finding a sweet little companion who would purr in her lap while she watched old episodes of *Friends* – and was now living this bullied, living-hell existence, controlled by fear. Maybe she didn't even like stew, or Parma violets!

All this, however, was by the bye. The main issue was not forgotten.

'Tetty, where's Watson?' I said. 'What have you done with him, and what do you want from me?'

She laughed, which was infuriating. 'Oh, keep your hair on,' she said.

'I will not keep my hair on,' I replied, somewhat nonsensically. 'I refuse point-blank to keep my hair on until you give me my dog back.'

'Suit yourself,' she said. 'But whether you keep your hair on or not, you won't see your precious Watson till after the job tomorrow night.'

The oddness of this form of words (in particular, the word 'job') sort of hung in the air until I dared to bring it down.

'Tetty, you're an incredibly successful villainess, aren't you?'

'I won't lie,' she said. 'Yeah, I am.' And then she added, 'Why do you ask?'

'Did you mastermind the Hatton Garden heist?'

She laughed and flexed her claws. 'There's not a soul could pin it on me,' she said (which I think was an admission).

'Well, look,' I said. 'If you're this villainess, it stands to reason you must have countless callous underworld minions just sitting around waiting to act in villainous ways at your command.'

'I got plenty of such callous minions, yeah.'

'Rough, tough, callous minions?'

'Yeah!' She sounded impatient. 'What you driving at?'

'If you've got rough, tough underworld minions, I don't understand! Why on earth do you need me?'

Tetty gave me a long, hard look, and then reached a decision.

'I was hoping to avoid this, dear,' she said, 'but we've got off on the wrong foot. You seem to think you're in a position to argue with me.'

Then she called to Mrs Fletcher, who entered holding something loosely wrapped in newspaper, and delivered it to me. And it was as if time stood still. I looked down at the paper parcel. It was very light in my hands. Mrs Fletcher grimaced at me, as if saying she was sorry. I noticed there was horror in her eyes.

I looked at Tetty. She put her head to one side. She purred. I looked down at the parcel.

'Open it,' she said.

I swallowed hard. I couldn't believe this was happening.

'Go on, dear,' she said. 'Watson would want you to have it.'

Oh my God. On her face was precisely the look of triumph and contempt I had seen before – when I'd found she had poisoned Watson in my kitchen.

What had she done?

'No, I can't,' I said.

She looked at Mrs Fletcher. 'Didn't I say that would happen?'

Mrs Fletcher nodded. 'You did, Kitty dear,' she said flatly.

'He won't open it!' Tetty laughed. 'Aren't you even curious about which ear it is? Perhaps it's both!'

I looked down at the newspaper. The faintest trace of a bloodstain was visible. At which awful sight I felt my face dissolve in misery. I had spent the last couple of days being absurdly brave and defiant about the threat to my own life posed by the Oviri – but the mere thought of someone hurting Watson had reduced me to Enforced Tetty Servitude in an instant. Those terrible words – '*Perhaps it's both!*'

'I'll do anything,' I said quietly. 'Just tell me, Tetty. Tell me what to do. Why would you want to hurt Watson?'

'Ooh, am I a *fiend,* dear?' she asked.

I'm afraid to say I broke down a little bit. 'Yes, you are!' I snivelled.

Tetty nodded to Mrs Fletcher, who picked up the wrapped object and took it out of the room again.

'Now,' said Tetty, looking at me gleefully. 'That's more like it. Oh, look at him! Look at his little face!'

As I discovered over the next half-hour or so, Tetty was not just a callously ambitious demon kitten; she was also mad. For some reason, this possibility had not previously occurred to me. All the evil talking cats I had encountered thus far had been extremely clever and deeply self-serving, but criminal insanity had not by any means been a distinguishing feature. True, the Captain had been violent and very scary: he had attacked and nearly killed Dr Winterton outside the library; he had then finished the job by smothering poor Winterton in his hospital bed. But Tetty was less the wild and savage beast, more the classic gangster psychopath. For example, after the evil exclamation 'Oh, look at him! Look at his little face!' she lay on her back on the floor, cackling, and played with a conveniently placed ball of sky-blue wool. It was shocking, and I looked away, but she laughed all the more at my discomfort. And then she howled like a dog – like a dog *in agony* – while all the time laughing at me and playing like a baby with the wool.

After such a display, getting information from me was absurdly easy. In no time she had got from me everything I knew about the origins of the Oviri, and about Roger's plan to stop her making a bargain with Beelzebub. I had anticipated that she would know of Roger's existence. I had expected his name to mean something to her. However, I hadn't realised she would hate him with such a passion. But when you look at the facts, it was logical that she would. She had five good reasons to regard him as her personal nemesis:

1. It was Roger that the Captain had always loved.
2. It was Roger's absconding from Harville Manor that had caused the whole evil-kitten experiment there – of which Tetty was the greatest success (and the lasting monument) – to collapse.
3. Because of Roger's defection, Tetty's beloved Cat Master, John Seeward, had hanged himself.
4. Because of Roger, the Captain had finally died down a well. And lastly,
5. Because of Roger, the all-important pamphlet *Nine Lives* had got into the wrong hands, necessitating the infiltration of the home

of this stupid retired librarian who thought he could outwit one of the cleverest cats that had ever lived by hiding the pamphlet behind some everyday Kellogg's products in a cupboard above the fridge.

'Tell me what you want from me,' I said again.

'Oh, not much,' she said. 'You're going to be the new Cat Master, that's all.'

Blimey. I hadn't seen that one coming.

'What?' I said.

'You heard,' she said. And then, effortlessly, she leapt across from the sofa to the arm of my chair, and looked straight up into my face, those huge kitten eyes close to mine. She tilted her head and began to purr. It was terrifying.

'Gah!' I said. I wanted to push her off, but I couldn't bear to touch her. Instead I shut my eyes, pressing myself deeper into the chair. 'Get off!' I said. 'Please get off.'

But when I opened my eyes again, she had leaned further towards me and her face was close to mine, those beady kitten eyes looking so innocent, so beguiling. The purr was now so insistent as to be extremely menacing.

'Stroke me, Alec,' she said.

'What?' I said.

'Go on. Stroke me.'

'No.'

'Oh Alec. Surely you know that all the scientific evidence suggests that the act of stroking a pussycat significantly reduces blood pressure?'

I made a mental note to send a small paper to the *British Medical Journal* if I got out of this alive, pointing out that the scientific evidence regarding cats and blood pressure perhaps needed to be looked at again. I wanted to shout, 'Tetty, are you *insane*?' but it's a well-known fact that psychopaths are touchy about words like 'mad' and 'crazy', and that you use such terms at your peril.

She placed a seductive paw on my arm.

'Hail, O new Cat Master,' she said. 'Go on, stroke me. I know you want to.'

Reluctantly obeying, I placed a cupped hand on the top of her head. The fur was soft. Her little ears were silky. I swallowed hard and told myself I could get through this – but then (oh God) she lifted herself, pressing her head up into my hand, and I pulled away in disgust. But she continued, pointedly, to purr, and purr, and purr – and in the end there was nothing for it. I lowered my hand again, took some deep breaths, and prepared to meet the disgusting animal pressure from Tetty with responding pressure of my own.

'Good boy, Alec,' she said as I touched her lightly again. 'Good boy. Oooh. That's it. Ooh, that's nice. Now the back, come on.'

So – well, I'm not proud of it. I did what I had to do.

'That's it,' she said, arching her neck again and going limp as I drew my hand lightly down her tiny fluffy (evil) body. 'Oh, yeah,' she said, dreamily. 'Yes, yes. Don't forget the tail! Oh yeah. That's it. Just there. Just *there*.'

Well, it was vile. I had to fight the impulse to shut my eyes, it was all so incredibly unpleasant. She whimpered and purred in response to my touch, and of course she continued to call the shots. At the end of it, I felt not only sullied and humiliated, but also alarmed. Forced cat-petting as a form of abuse! *Whatever evil thing would this demonic kitten think of next?*

'Hail, O Cat Master,' she said again at last, breathily.

She seemed satisfied. I tried not to think about it.

'Can we stop now?' I pleaded.

'For the time being,' she said.

'Oh, thank God,' I said. 'Thank God.'

I wondered if the stroking session might have mellowed her a little, so I spoke gently to her.

'Tetty,' I said. 'Dear little Tetty.'

She looked at me sideways, suspicious.

'Tetty, I can't possibly be Cat Master, can I? I mean, *me*?' I laughed at the thought of it. 'Me?' I repeated. 'Tetty, you must be *mad*.'

Oops. I had inadvertently used the 'm' word.

'Mad?' she repeated.

I pressed on, quickly. 'It's just, why on earth would you want me to be the Cat Master?' I blurted. 'There must be better people than me. I'd be hopeless.'

'Precisely!' she said. 'Now, look at me, Alec. Come on. That's right, look me in the eye.'

I obeyed her. Her huge, unblinking eyes fixed mine, and she spoke slowly and clearly, so that I would take it all in. 'I will only say this once,' she said. 'In all my born days, I have never met anyone less suited to be a Cat Master than you. You haven't got one iota of criminal spark, have you?'

I didn't mind admitting this. 'No, I haven't,' I said.

'You haven't got one jot of ambition.'

This seemed a bit unfair. I had, after all, beaten two rivals to the job of periodicals librarian back in 1989, but I let it go. When Tetty talked of ambitions, she probably meant ambitions less in the sense of leapfrogging a couple of civil service pay grades, more in the sense of world domination. So I said 'No' again.

'And to top it all,' she said, 'you are as honest as the day is long!'

This was true, too.

'In other words,' she concluded, 'you're perfect! You'll be like putty in my hands!'

At this she yawned and stretched, patted my arm, and then jumped back to her sofa. Mrs Fletcher returned with the golden bowl and set it on the floor. This time, Tetty jumped down (so prettily!) and neatly ate the caviar with many 'Mmmm' noises, her little head bent over the bowl, showing the beautiful ginger fluff between her ears. Seeing her in this vulnerable position, I have to admit I felt a strong desire to kill her with my bare hands, but I knew I couldn't. I knew the risk to Watson was too great.

'Roger never told me what happened there at Harville in the fifties,' I said when she had finished and was back on the sofa again.

'Ooh, are you hoping I'll tell you my story, dear?' she said, laughing. 'Hoping I might *weep*?'

'No,' I said. 'I'm just curious. There are lots of things I want to know. For example, have you read Timkins's journal?'

Tetty stopped laughing. In fact, the mere mention of Timkins's journal had an extraordinary effect.

'How *could* you?' she demanded. She gasped and turned away from me; raising a paw, she seemed to be wiping tears from her eyes.

'Tetty, are you all right?' I said, getting up.

'Oh, sit down, sit down,' she said, recovering herself. 'Now then, where were we?'

'I expect you don't want to talk about it,' I said carefully. She had definitely been unnerved.

'No, I bleeding don't!'

'Poor Timkins,' I said. But she was not to be drawn, and she flashed a warning look at me, so I desisted.

Should I leave? I wondered. It did seem that our ghastly business was complete. It also seemed that the way forward was inescapable. I was to return the following night, offer myself to the Devil's service in perpetuity (as a surprise Christmas present), sign the relevant forms, and spend the rest of my life operating in a managerial capacity under the thumb of a ruthless baby animal weighing less than a couple of pounds, who could always (oh, horror!) *make me stroke her whether I wanted to or not.*

'Well, if that's all for now,' I said, rising.

But I was wrong. Tetty's mood swings were extraordinary. 'Where do you think you're going, Farnsbarns?' she snapped.

'But Roger will be looking for me,' I said.

She pulled a face, as if to say, *Am I bothered?*

'He wants to stop you!' I said. 'And he's very clever! It won't take him long to find me.'

She seemed genuinely unconcerned. 'Oh, don't go worrying about *'im,*' she said darkly. 'We've all got our weak spots.'

I pondered this, but I couldn't make sense of it. Did Roger really have any weak spots? Did he care about anyone the way I cared about Watson? Then again, there was so much I didn't know about Roger. In fact it pained me that there were so many gaps. When he had offhandedly mentioned his theory about who might have rescued him from the well and bundled him off to the Greek islands, it wasn't just frustrated curiosity that I'd felt. I had felt jealous. About Roger's life I wanted to know everything.

'Once you're the Cat Master,' Tetty explained, 'we can deal with the likes of Roger. In fact, he's number one on the agenda. There's been a lot of loose ends over the years, if you get my meaning. Loose ends that need chopping off. Those bleeding useless Lunar cats, for starters.'

'They were Timkins's friends,' I pointed out.

Again, it was the wrong thing to say. 'Not one of them lifted a claw to help him!' she replied hotly. Timkins was evidently a very sensitive subject as far as Tetty was concerned.

A sensible person would have dropped it. But it turns out that – hopeless as I am in so many respects that might qualify a person for a career in criminality – I can never stop asking questions, even when I've been told to shut up in no uncertain terms. Thus I found myself going on.

'I suppose it was Timkins himself – I mean, the Captain – who told you about the Oviri?'

She huffed with impatience. 'Of course it was! Who else knew?'

I sensed her anger, but I still couldn't let the subject go. 'So why now? If you've known about it for nearly sixty years, why dig it up now? Why not before?'

'For crying out loud. Because it belonged to the Captain!'

'Oh.'

'And he didn't bleeding well want it dug up, did he?' To be honest, this was explanation enough, but I seemed to have touched such a raw nerve that she ranted on, 'Until I was sure he'd really gone for good, I wouldn't touch it, dear. I couldn't and I wouldn't!'

'Right. Well, that makes sense. Thank you.'

'When you think what he'd been through on account of that fucking thing!'

'Right, yes. Exactly. Dear oh dear. But it's done now. We could change the subject if you like.'

'That whole fucking voyage!'

'I know. Tsk.'

'Three years!'

'I know, yes.'

'All those friends of his, *fucking dead*.'

It was ironic that I had wanted her to open up, but now that she was worked up, I seriously wished I could stop her. Things were getting out of hand. There was a strange low buzzing noise in the air.

And for the first time that evening, I had felt a proper tug on my ankle – a serious throbbing tug.

'Tetty, shouldn't you calm down?'

'And when he finally realised Hawkesworth never believed in him as a scientist at all—'

'What? Didn't he?'

'No, of course not! He didn't believe in any of them as scientists. It was all a ruse from the start. He played those Lunar cats like a cheap pianola. He'd heard tell of the Oviri, see, when he was researching one of his so-called "Eastern Tales", and he became obsessed with the thought of it. It was like an Eastern Tale in itself, the way the thought of that Oviri filled all his dreams at night, drove him crazy with ambition. "I could compete with the very Devil if I had that doll," he said to himself.'

For the first time, I wished the Lunar cats had been there, so that one of them could make a useful note. On the other hand, Tetty's 'cheap pianola' simile might have been painful for them to hear.

'So he thought, I'll just humour these cats, I will,' Tetty continued. 'I'll encourage those silly, pretentious cats, with their formal gatherings and their worthless experiments; I'll print up their proceedings and whatnot; and then one day there'll be another voyage to the South Seas and I can smuggle one of them on board, telling him he's doing it for science! Can you imagine? He chose Timkins because he was the most amenable, but also because (and I'm sad to say this) he was the most susceptible to flattery. Poor Timkins. It was bad enough to find out the Cat Master had sent him all that way just to collect that evil thing; but then one day he says to Timkins – he says it *right out* – "You thought you'd solve the longitude problem, did you? Well, what a joke. You're a *cat*, Timkins. Never forget that you're *just a cat*! And by the way, your journals were too terrible to use as part of my great work. When I told you they were damaged beyond repair, it was just to save your feelings. They were rubbish, Timkins. Absolute, stinking, awful feline rubbish."'

Well, I had heard a few things to old Hawkesworth's discredit over the past couple of days, but I have to say, this revelation of Tetty's took things to a new level.

'That's shocking,' I said. '"Feline rubbish"?'

'That's what he said,' said Tetty, sniffing. '*Stinking* feline rubbish.'

'Poor Timkins,' I said, aware that I was repeating myself. But this time Tetty responded, as if grateful for my sympathy.

'Poor Timkins,' she agreed.

And for a brief moment there, I felt that we were united in historical compassion. In fact, if Tetty hadn't throughout these proceedings been deliberately breaking my heart – by holding my small, beloved, innocent doggie for purposes of extortion, while also proposing to enslave me to a lifetime's servitude as Revolted Powerless Kitten-Petter in Chief – I might have felt a real bond.

It was at this point that something unexpected happened. I was just about to tell Tetty about the new developments in my ankle area when Mrs Fletcher came in from the kitchen, looking concerned.

'Kittykins,' she said. 'I don't know how to tell you this.'

'What?' said Tetty.

'The dolly thing. It's got loose. I don't know where it is.'

'What? But how—'

'I don't know!' said Mrs Fletcher. 'It was in its box half an hour ago, but I did notice the box was rocking.'

Tetty looked at me accusingly, and I was about to be helpful and draw attention to the strange buzzing noise when I felt another tug on my ankle – such a forceful tug, in fact, that I almost fell out of my chair.

'Oh no,' I said. And then, 'Oh, not yet; please God, not yet.'

Then the phone rang, and Mrs Fletcher ran to answer it, while Tetty, furious, launched a violent slashing attack on the arm of the sofa she was sitting on, producing a veritable snowstorm of upholstery foam. I suppose to someone of Tetty's criminally insane mindset, pointless violence is good for venting feelings, but I couldn't see how otherwise it was helpful in the circumstances to destroy a perfectly good piece of Multiyork loungeware. Meanwhile my leg, beyond my conscious control, was oscillating back and forth, and the lavender bag had been shaken off.

Tetty was rattled. 'You!' she said suddenly, accusingly. 'Did you do this?'

This was so ridiculous that I almost laughed. 'How could I have done? I've just been sitting here the whole time. And apart from anything else, *why* would I? It wants to kill me! Look at my leg, Tetty! Look!'

But Tetty shushed me. She wanted to hear Mrs Fletcher on the phone. Personally, I was torn between wanting to hear what Mrs Fletcher was saying, and worrying that I might die within the next couple of minutes. I had noticed, you see, that the feather-light stuffing Tetty had ripped from the arm of the sofa was lifting up into the air, and that the buzzing noise was louder.

'What?' Mrs Fletcher was saying in disbelief. 'Speak up, I can't hear you. But how? Oh Deirdre, she won't like this. She really won't like this!'

Tetty yelled, 'What's happened?'

Mrs Fletcher put down the phone. 'Someone's taken the dog,' she called.

For a moment we all held our positions, just attempting to take it all in. If I had to label how I was feeling at that moment, I'd say that I felt terror, but I also felt hope. I felt this was likely to be the end, but I also felt that I would quite like the end to come soon, all things considered. However, when the lavender bag with all the hairy tape attached to it gently rose from the floor and started to circle the room along with the assorted flecks and chunks of white padding material from the sofa, my mixed emotions were quickly reduced to just one overwhelming sense: a sense of impending doom.

'This is it,' I said. 'Tell Watson I love him!'

'Oh, shut up and let me think,' said Tetty.

But more and more of the lighter objects in the room were rising. Tetty, feeling herself lift off the sofa, called to Mrs Fletcher, 'Hold me, for God's sake.' I wanted to run, but my leg had turned to lead, and while I struggled to move it I found that my vision was clouding with a sort of red mist, and I could hear weird birdsong and I felt incredibly hot. The smell of warm earth and dank vegetation nearly choked me, and strange words started coming from my mouth, and then I heard – unmistakably – the dread noise Timkins had heard so often on the ship: the knocking of the wooden idol as it made its stealthy way across a wooden floor.

There was, believe it or not, one small pleasure to be savoured in this by-and-large-terrible moment. That damned Oviri was ruining Tetty's plans, and she was incandescent. Pressed against the chest of Mrs Fletcher, she was yelling, uselessly, 'Get back in your box! I'm ordering you to get back in your box!'

And then the front door swung open and it was as if the whole scene froze. I found I was floating in silence next to the ceiling and looking down on a tableau: Roger at full stretch in mid-air, as he magnificently leapt into the room at the head of the excited Lunar cats; Wiggy to his right, leading my darling Watson, who was caught standing on his hind legs mid-bark (and all-importantly, thank heaven, with both ears still attached). Wiggy's sleeve, I noticed, was rolled up – and when I saw that on his hand was a fully formed mouthey-mouthey, precisely similar to the one on my ankle (oh no), I wanted to shout at him to hide it, but of course this wasn't happening in real time so I couldn't.

Debris hovered. Lights were dim. The man in the armchair (which was me) had his face in his hands and his left leg held high, as if waiting for a bird to land on it; Tetty's face was contorted with annoyance; Mrs Fletcher's eyes were closed. And while this scene was held in perfect suspension, a small, dark, wooden object rose from the floor in the corner of the room and began to move. Slowly and steadily it travelled towards its sitting-duck target in the armchair (i.e. me).

'Woof!' said Watson as the spell broke and the vortex in the room began to spin again.

'No!' I shouted.

'Alec!' said Roger.

'Stop this!' commanded Tetty.

'Woof, woof, woof!' barked Watson.

Everything in the room was vibrating. The Lunar cats sent up a tremendous unearthly wailing noise, led by Signor Andreotti, which might have been helpful, but I'm not sure it was. Principally, it just made everything else much harder to hear.

'Take me, not him!' Wiggy yelled, and flung himself in the path of the Oviri.

'What, are you mad?' I said.

'Alec, this can't happen to you!' he said. 'I'm always the early victim! It's OK!'

'No!' I said. 'Wiggy, you can't!'

'Stop this, you bleeders!' shouted Tetty.

'Look out!' said Roger as the Oviri swerved in its course, as if taking Wiggy at his word.

And then, just as I was reaching for Wiggy to push him away, I noticed that Watson, off the lead, had run and leapt into the air.

Oh no.

'Watson, don't!' I shouted. 'Stop it! Don't!' But before anyone could do anything, he had caught the Oviri between his jaws.

'Stop that!' Tetty shouted, but she had even less control over Watson than she did over anything else in this situation.

All the stuff in the air started spinning faster and more forcefully. Pictures were ripped off the walls and a standard lamp fell over. Tetty jumped down from Mrs Fletcher's arms and appeared to flee.

'Take me with you!' shouted Mrs Fletcher.

'Not blooming likely!' was the reply from the departing kitten.

But no one took any notice. All eyes were, understandably, on my idiot of a dog, who had evidently mistaken an airborne ancient Tahitian idol for a new and interesting kind of Frisbee.

'Drop it, Watson,' I said in my most commanding voice. 'Drop it now!' But, as usual, my commanding voice had no effect, and Watson shook the Oviri like a rat, while it emitted a piercing scream, and some of the wallpaper was torn from the walls to join the already dangerously crowded maelstrom of domestic objects circling above our heads.

'Watson, no!' I ordered him. But he merely shook the Oviri again, a bit harder, and the scream increased.

'Stop him, Alec,' said Roger.

'I'm trying!' I said.

And then Watson shook the Oviri for a third time, and quite suddenly the screaming stopped (it was like the sound of a bagpipe deflating), and all the stuff in the air stopped spinning and rained heavily to the ground, so that everyone was saying 'Ouch!' and 'Ow!' and 'What?' and a couple of the Lunar cats did sustain minor injuries from quite big ornaments dropping on their heads, but they never complained afterwards at all, which was typical of their generally selfless attitude.

Watson looked pleased with himself. The rest of us needed a moment or two to believe the danger was truly over. But it seemed clear that it was. For one thing, my leg felt normal. Watson prodded at the lifeless Oviri, then he sniffed it, and then, I'm afraid to say, he spread himself across it and urinated on it, which is one of those animal assertion behaviours I have learned to expect from my dear Watson, and which I felt in the circumstances I could (for once) wholeheartedly condone, even though we were indoors. He looked up at me from the floor with his tongue hanging out, and then jumped up on my lap to say how much he'd missed me.

'Oh Watson,' I gasped. 'Good dog. Good dog.' My little dog had shaken to death an object so evil that the Devil himself had desired to own it. He had routed a kitten whose cunning was matched only by her mental instability. He had literally brought the house down. I have to say, I felt extremely proud.

Part Four

Chapter Six

There are few things more enjoyable than wrapping up a story. Over the next hour or two – with the threat from the Oviri evaporated, and with Tetty out of the picture – we had a pleasant time tying up loose ends, and reliving (in the safety of retrospection) the many alarming moments we had endured over the past few days. With relief came other emotions. The Lunar cats, for example, had the leisure now to experience guilt and sorrow about Timkins (because it was sadly true, as Tetty had screamed at me, that they had *never lifted a claw to help him*). Roger was generally contented with how things had turned out, but still cross with me for taking matters into my own hands vis-à-vis the hostage situation. Wiggy was insanely relieved not to be starting the backstage party in the Great Old Dressing Room in the Sky. Watson was very pleased to be back with me again, and celebrated by falling asleep with his tongue hanging out and all four legs in the air. Mr Bruise, as a way of expressing some long-pent-up emotions, punched a large hole in a wall.

As for me, however, I could not relax. There was still so much to know. How had Tetty controlled Mrs Fletcher? Where was Timkins's journal? Where was the *Nine Lives* pamphlet? Would I still have to be Cat Master? How could a ghastly mouthey-mouthey thing just appear on one's ankle and then disappear again without trace? How could one reconcile the sweet and curious Timkins with the terrifying Captain of the later years, who willingly helped in the creation of evil kittens such as Tetty as a master weapon to be used against mankind?

Surprisingly, it was Mrs Fletcher who turned out to be the source for much of this information. She handed over both the journal and the *Nine Lives* pamphlet at once. I have hinted already that this somewhat generic (and nasty) old woman was someone who might repay closer inspection – and so it proved. With Tetty gone, this interesting female burst into tears, and we all saw with amazement that she was indeed not a particularly old (or nasty) woman at all. As I had previously guessed, she was in her late forties. When she stood up straight and looked us in the eye – instead of bending almost double and studying the floor – she was even quite nice-looking! It turned out that she had met Tetty just a few months before, when the kitten had appeared to be in peril in the middle of a busy road in Bromley. 'She was mewing on a traffic island,' she explained to us. 'I rescued her! I thought she was a poor little stray!'

What had subsequently happened Mrs Fletcher found difficult to relate. I suppose it's embarrassing to admit to being so efficiently oppressed by a furball who weighs about the same as an economy packet of tissues. I was suspecting that Tetty had employed blackmail, or some sort of torture of a supernatural nature: how else could a mere kitten control a human being so completely, bending her to her evil will? Well, the answer is about as fiendish as you can imagine. Tetty had targeted Mrs Fletcher. She'd known she was not only a widow but a cat lover of long standing, temporarily without any cats. Having infiltrated Mrs Fletcher's home, she had done the one thing that would make a well-meaning but emotionally needy cat person turn to putty in her hands. She had simply looked into the face of Mrs Fletcher one day and declared, 'I love you.'

When the poor woman told us this, we all gasped. Oh, this was beyond evil. This was *enormity*. Roger was so astonished that he spluttered, 'Will that kitten stop at nothing?'

'I know!' Mrs Fletcher wept. 'I know I shouldn't have believed her! But all my life I've had cats, you see; and I've said to them, "I love you, I love you, I love you," and they have never . . .' She faltered, and tried again. 'They have *never* . . .' But she still couldn't get it out.

'Of course they have never said they loved you!' snapped Roger. 'Because it would be a lie!'

'But you can't imagine how much I wanted to hear it, all the same!'

Well, what a shockingly fiendish cat Tetty was, as regards exploiting the pitiable neediness of a Mrs Fletcher. I suddenly realised there was a gap in the market for a self-help book entitled *Cats Who*

Don't Care About Anybody, and the Women Who Love Them. Tetty hadn't done it all at once, either. She hadn't rushed into saying 'I love you' to Mrs Fletcher. This craftiest of creatures had, it seems, worked up to it slowly and methodically. First she'd had to let Mrs Fletcher know she could talk; then there had been a couple of weeks' grace while Mrs Fletcher had got used to that. But then one day Mrs Fletcher had put down Tetty's food, and the kitten had said, 'Oh, that's very kind of you, Mrs F.'

I noticed that all the cats were very uncomfortable hearing this. For a cat to say thank you to a human was a betrayal of every cat code of behaviour by which the Lunar cats had lived for nearly 250 years. In fact, it is a betrayal of the code of all cats, at all times, everywhere. Which is why Tetty's devilish scheme had been so effective.

'And then she started to say proper thank-yous,' said Mrs Fletcher.

A frisson of revulsion and disapproval rippled through the Lunar cats.

'And then one day I was cuddling her in front of the TV and she looked up at me and said, "Has anyone ever told you you're a very nice person?" And then a couple of days after that she scratched me quite badly and then she said she was sorry, and I said, "Oh, I love you, Kitty," and she said . . .' Mrs Fletcher stopped. There was a catch in her voice. 'She said, "I love you, too,"' she continued bravely. 'And then she said – oh God, she really said this! She said, "And I really miss you when you're not in the house"!'

The poor woman. To have been subjected to such naked, enormous, pernicious fibs! And yet you couldn't blame her for becoming enslaved; for believing what she wanted to believe. After decades of ministering to cats who behaved in the usual offhand, superior fashion, Tetty had seemed like the answer to all her prayers: a cat who embodied gratitude and affection; who actually took note of whether she was at home or at the shops!

By the time Mrs Fletcher shared this with us, we were all back at the hotel. Wiggy, I noticed, kept nodding off. But Mrs Fletcher was keen to get everything off her chest: how she had helped Tetty dig in the churchyard; how she and Tetty had found there in the earth an old rusted capsule containing not only the Oviri but Timkins's journal, miraculously preserved; how Tetty had read the journal and then talked about the Captain with such pain and sorrow. Evidently the original plan for Tetty, when she was recruited by the Captain in the 1950s, had been that she would work crimes in a team, alongside an older cat like Roger – but when the Harville experiment was terminated, she had run away and formed an east London gang with other rough kittens, and then – bit by bit – she had climbed over the upturned faces of her backstabbed gangland rivals and finally become the unscrupulous feline Top Cat of today.

I got a chance to look at Timkins's journal. It was indeed a painful document. Roger sat reading it with tears rolling down his face; the Lunar cats gave way to uncontrollable howling. Roger had known the worst of the Captain but he had also known the best. What struck him most on reading his old friend's journal was that it was the Captain's loyalty that had been his frequent undoing. He had been betrayed by Hawkesworth in 1773; two centuries later, it was his loyalty to Seeward and Prideaux that had brought him to his end.

'When did he become the Captain?' I asked. 'I mean, when did he drop the name Timkins?'

'Immediately after the death of Hawkesworth,' said Roger, 'when he went to sea again. Some of the sailors on his first ship had been crew on the *Endeavour* and they gave him the name ironically, but over time it fitted him more and more. He bulked up in size. He got stronger. Despite all he had gone through, he decided he preferred the rough honesty of sailors to the cruel double-dealing he had experienced on land. Also, of course, he didn't fancy being anywhere in the vicinity of the Oviri again, whether buried in the churchyard or not.'

'Was he a good sailor, in the end?' I asked.

'The best,' said Roger proudly. 'His navigational skills were tremendous, it turned out. He sailed the world for the next hundred and forty years, leaving behind many legends. And he wasn't alone. There was a whole fraternity of ship's cats that he used to talk to me about: canny, clever cats who would meet at ports around the globe, swapping songs and stories – so many stories, of voyages and typhoons and Malayan rubber planters and men-who-would-be-kings. Listening to the Captain was like listening to a cross between Rudyard Kipling, Joseph Conrad, H. G. Wells and Somerset Maugham. It is incredibly tragic that at the age of two hundred and forty-eight, he ended up dead down a well in Dorset.'

I nodded. It was the first time I had felt the real loss of the Captain. Up to now, I had continued to bear in mind that he had killed a friend of mine in a grotesque fashion, had demolished a portion of the library I used to work in, and had also been directly instrumental in the death of my dear wife Mary.

'In the end, the Captain had one special friend: the cat who sailed on Ernest Shackleton's *Endurance* to the Antarctic – a splendid, bold tabby tom whose real name was Benjamin, but who was known on the *Endurance* as "Mrs Chippy", because it was the ship's carpenter who befriended him. The Captain and Benjamin travelled together for twenty years! Even when they took jobs separately, they looked out for each other. It was the Captain, for example, who advised Benjamin not to travel on the Franklin expedition. It was Benjamin who made the Captain promise never to sail on the *Lusitania* if war with Germany broke out – a promise the Captain remembered on the very day the ship was due to sail from New York.'

'What happened to Benjamin?' I asked. I had a feeling this was going to be a story without a happy ending.

'He was shot,' said Roger. 'Shot by Shackleton himself.'

'What?' said Wiggy (waking up).

'Whatever for?' I asked. 'What had he done?'

Roger shrugged. 'There's a case for saying it was necessary,' he said. 'The ship was stuck in ice and breaking up. The crew had to abandon ship and make their way across frozen terrain with boats and dogs. Shackleton always boasted afterwards that at least he got every man back to safety – but by some he was never forgiven for killing poor Benjamin.'

'Excuse me, when was this, please?' asked a Lunar cat, who was taking notes.

'1915.'

'Thank you.'

'When the rescued crew of the *Endurance* returned to Britain, of course, the Captain joined the crowds that went to greet them. Can you imagine? It was only then that he learned that his great friend had been sacrificed. The Captain was devastated. He and Benjamin had been planning to set up a boarding house for retired ship's cats near Putney Bridge. It was when he was at this low ebb (and not at sea) that he was picked up by the Cat Master of the day, and drawn back into the violent and horrible recruitment and training of evil talking cats – which was how he met me, of course, in 1927.'

I stepped in. 'And you both ran away to sea, didn't you?'

'We did.' Roger looked wistfully into the middle distance. 'His whole life was about putting oceans between himself and the Cat Masters.'

The Lunar cats hissed at the mention of Cat Masters. Roger acknowledged this strength of feeling by raising his eyebrow whiskers, and then continued.

'He had no sooner recruited me than he wanted to save me, so off we went, on our Grand Tour, which only stopped when I was kidnapped in Athens and brought back to London. The Captain searched for me everywhere, and then finally came back to England himself – where, once again, he was exploited by . . . *Cat Masters*.'

This time he really milked it. At the very words 'Cat' and 'Masters', there was a general hiss of horror.

This prompted a small memory that had been nagging at me. Was it time to say something? From a good-manners point of view, I felt it was wrong to turn the subject round to myself, when everyone was engrossed in the Captain. However, I decided I must speak up.

'Roger, there's something I didn't tell you about Tetty's plans.'

'What?' he said. 'Can it wait until morning now? We're all getting quite tired.'

'I don't know. It might be important.' I hesitated. It was this talk of Cat Masters that had made me think of it. 'It's just that she was having a meeting tomorrow night with Beelzebub.'

'Yes. We knew that.'

'She was going to deliver the Oviri to him.'

'Yes.'

'And in return he was going to restore the succession of Cat Masters.'

'Was he?'

Roger looked puzzled, and a little annoyed. This was new information, and I could see by the way he immediately shot a quizzical glance at Mrs Fletcher that he couldn't quite picture her in the job. I took a deep breath. It was time to risk a big laugh of derision from all concerned.

'The thing is, I know you'll laugh, but the new Cat Master she was proposing – well, it was me.'

But only Wiggy laughed. He emitted a loud 'Ha!' – and then stopped abruptly when he realised the others had taken it very seriously. Roger closed his eyes, the better to concentrate.

'Ah,' he breathed at last.

'Ah,' echoed the Lunar cats, although some of them looked uncertain about what was going on. I heard an 'Mm' and a *miaow* as well. Mr Tinkle nervously crossed his legs.

This was quite worrying.

'Why did you say "Ah" like that?' I asked. 'It's nothing to worry about, is it? I mean, now that Tetty's gone and the meeting won't take place, and she can't make me do it?'

Roger didn't reply. He pulled a face; a face that I had, regrettably, seen before. He didn't need to say the words 'Alec, it isn't quite as simple as that'. I could just tell that was what he was thinking.

'Do you know if she named you on the form?' he said at last.

I shook my head. 'I've no idea,' I said. 'What form?'

Mrs Fletcher piped up. 'I helped her fill in a form,' she said.

We all turned to look at her. She reached for her handbag and retrieved a folded piece of paper. She unfolded it, and scanned it. 'I don't think anyone was named,' she was saying. 'No,' she said, refolding it again. 'No one is named. She said no to the catering. That was sensible. But oh, didn't she lie through her teeth about there being no parking difficulties!'

She realised she'd said too much. 'No one was named, no,' she repeated. 'Does that help?'

'Yes, that's good,' said Roger.

'Yes, that's good,' echoed the Lunar cats, cluelessly, with additional mutterings of 'That's very good, surely', 'That's excellent', 'What a relief' and 'Hoorah.'

Roger turned to me. 'Alec, I need you to think. Did you leave anything at all in that house?' he asked. 'Anything that could be traced back to you? Anything, especially, that would have your DNA?'

I thought about it. I couldn't remember taking anything there, or leaving anything either. As for DNA, no one had offered me a cup of tea or anything. I certainly hadn't licked the walls. Roger's urgent questioning was beginning to make me feel I'd been a bit stupid not to mention all this before. Now that I thought about it properly, moreover, I realised he was right.

'Come on, think!' he said.

'I am thinking, Roger.'

'What time was Beelzebub due to arrive?' he said, changing the subject.

'I don't know, but definitely after dark, because she talked about the full moon.'

'Midnight,' said Mrs F, holding up the piece of paper. 'But not tonight. Tomorrow.'

Roger jumped up and signalled to the other cats. They exchanged glances, excitedly. Wiggy and I both got up, too. Mrs Fletcher reached for her coat.

'No, you humans stay here,' Roger told me. He turned to the Lunar cats. 'Fancy a spot of organised purring?' he said with a smile. And they all cheered and followed him out of the room, as usual getting temporarily stuck in the doorway when they all tried to get through at once.

Left to our own devices, we humans weren't sure what to do with ourselves. Speaking for myself, it was the first time I'd been addressed as 'you humans', and I wasn't sure I approved. But I felt I had been stupid, not mentioning the Cat Master issue before, so I wasn't in a good position to object about anything. Wiggy was clearly exhausted (although refusing to lie down). Mrs Fletcher was likewise very tired and drained, so I made her a cup of tea, using the hotel's mini-kettle. We considered switching on the TV, but rejected it. News of the real world would be too distracting, and would also seem profoundly irrelevant if it didn't contain stories about cats.

Watching Mrs F finally relax in an armchair with a cup of tea, I realised that I felt sorry for her involvement in all this. It was shocking that she had allowed Tetty to exploit her so easily, but, on the other hand, I had only to think back to the ghastly petting-under-compulsion session I had myself endured to acknowledge Tetty's brilliance in getting people to do things against their will. So there was compassion for Mrs Fletcher, competing with contempt. And then there was a sort of murderous anger as well, of course, when you considered that she had aided Tetty in first poisoning and then kidnapping my blameless little dog; and also when you remembered that she had (in my own kitchen!) clocked me on the head with a heavy book on loan from a venerable literary collection in the north-west corner of St James's Square.

As if reading my thoughts, Mrs F apologised. 'I'm very sorry for everything, Alec,' she said. 'I've been so weak.'

'Yes, you have,' I said. (I know this was harsh, but, as Bertie Wooster might have said, *I meant it to sting.*)

'I shouldn't have let her take me over like that. But she was so clever. She made me believe I was so worthless and inferior that no one else would ever put up with me. She made me feel I was just lucky that *she* would put up with me!'

Wiggy interrupted. 'Alec makes me feel like that sometimes,' he said unexpectedly.

I looked round. 'What?' I said.

He pulled a face. 'Sorry, Alec. But you do.'

'I was always trying to please her,' Mrs F went on. 'I ended up with no self-esteem at all. When those Lunar cats of yours made my house fall down, Tetty blamed *me* – and because she blamed me I blamed myself; I believed it was all my fault, even while I knew it wasn't. It was awful what she did to me – all while telling me she loved me. She told me I was stupid, even though I knew I couldn't be really. I used to say to myself, "What's happening to you, Lucy? Until last month you were deputy head of the English department at the University of Kent!" It was driving me mad. The basic thing was: I felt I would put up with anything rather than lose her, because I was so lucky that she loved me at all.'

I wished I could say something of comfort. But she didn't wait long enough for me to think what it would be.

'Anyway,' Mrs F concluded, 'I just wanted you to know I was never comfortable about attacking you in the shop, or knocking you unconscious, or any of the other things.'

'What was in that awful parcel?' I asked. It had suddenly come back to me: the folded newspaper she had placed in my hands at the house in Chislehurst Gardens.

'Oh,' she said. 'I put a bit of an old glove of mine in there; I stuffed it with some hair from my hairbrush to get the weight just so. Tetty knew I could never hurt an animal, whatever the situation. She didn't even try to talk me into it. She told me to put something else in the parcel. Like she said, she knew you wouldn't be able to look inside anyway.'

'I was terrified,' I said.

'I know. I'm sorry.'

'It was the worst feeling I've ever had.'

'I know.'

It was at this point that Wiggy raised a very important question. 'Why did Roger ask about DNA?'

But, sadly, Mrs Fletcher came up with a different question at the same time, and I preferred to answer that one. (It might conceivably be true, I realise as I write this, that I sometimes treat Wiggy as if he's an idiot.)

'What do you think they're doing at my sister's house?' was Mrs F's question.

'Ooh, destroying it, I expect,' I said cheerfully. 'Just like they destroyed your house the other day.'

Mrs Fletcher looked very glum, and I felt a little pulse of triumph. It wasn't much of a punishment for what she had done, but the next time she applied for buildings insurance, she was, surely, completely stuffed.

Wiggy piped up. 'It's amazing they're so good at it, you know. This precision-demolition-purring thing. They only tried it once before, when they had a group trip to Venice in the 1900s.'

'They went to Venice?' I said. 'I would have thought there were enough cats in Venice already.'

'So you might think. But Mr Nolly was telling me earlier that actually none of Venice's own cats, for all their snooty north Italian ways, had ever succeeded in bringing down the Campanile by orchestrated purring. All the Venetian cats had ever managed, he said, was setting fire to the Fenice Theatre, and that doesn't impress anybody any more because they've done the same thing so many times.'

It took a moment for this to sink in. I had seen pictures of the collapsed Campanile: a great heap of bricks with Edwardian Venetians standing alongside looking very tiny and scratching their heads in puzzlement.

'The Lunar cats brought down the Campanile in St Mark's Square?' I said.

'Nolly said they placed ashtrays from Florian's around the area where they predicted the rubble would fall, and they got it right to within a couple of inches. It was such a triumph they didn't bother to try it again. But it made them legends in Venice. Roger is going to take them back to Venice when this is all over, for a bit of a holiday. Now that the Oviri is vanquished, they have to decide what to do next with their lives.'

I was confused. How did Wiggy know all this? When had there been time for Roger and the Lunar cats to make holiday plans?

'We got chatting after you made your grand exit earlier this evening. Roger made us wait for a while before recovering Watson from Mrs Fletcher's sister and rescuing you from Tetty. So we got talking. They've waited a long time to find out what happened to Timkins, you know. They've all stayed in the area, living with families and so on, and then disappearing overnight and breaking people's hearts – because obviously, if they stayed for thirty or forty years with the same family, people would get suspicious about them never ageing. You remember how on the telly a local man said that the family cat had just disappeared, as if responding to a signal? That was Mr Tinkle! When Tetty and Mrs Fletcher here started the digging in the churchyard, all the Lunar cats got back together, from far and wide. It was like *Avengers Assemble* or something – only it was in Bromley, and it was without superpowers, or . . .' He stopped.

'Or much of a plan?' I offered.

'That's right,' said Wiggy. 'It was like *Avengers Assemble* except that it was in Bromley, and without superpowers, or anything resembling a plan.'

I suddenly realised I was tired. I lay back on one of the single beds in our room and let impressions of the day swim into my mind. Was it only that morning that the back of Wiggy's hand had been stuck fast to my ankle in the churchyard? Then there had been the awkward conversation with the vicar concerning imitation vomit; the amazing meeting with Roger; the whole epic tale of Timkins unfolded to us, with the sting of the sea on our faces and the crack of the sails above our heads; the terrible voicemails on my mobile phone as I sat in the darkened car on my own; the whirlwind of foam and strips of wallpaper whizzing around a living room as the Oviri launched itself at me while Tetty fruitlessly commanded it to stop. I thought of the Captain waiting expectantly at the docks for his long-dead friend; I thought of my absolute terror that Watson had been hurt; I thought of a 'form' inviting the Devil to a meeting in a house in Bromley; and Roger mentioning DNA – why *had* he mentioned DNA? And then something whizzed through my dreamy consciousness a few times, as if to say 'remember me' (or perhaps 'you've forgotten me'), and I suddenly sat up again.

'The lavender bag,' I said.

At which point, in the distance, we heard a muffled 'boom' as a house collapsed in Chislehurst Gardens.

So that explains why I am writing this on a train heading south from Paris in the middle of the night. Escaping en masse to Venice was as good a plan as any. Beside me on my left is Wiggy, asleep. Across the aisle is Mrs Fletcher, asleep. On the seat beside me on the other side is Watson, asleep. In the bags above our heads are a dozen clever eighteenth-century cats who (under expert guidance from the well-travelled Roger) bypassed all the security equipment at Ashford International and slipped aboard before the whistle blew. We are also carrying the *Nine Lives* pamphlet and the defunct Oviri, because Roger knows a shady, benighted spot in the Venetian lagoon where we can sink them together permanently in the mud. We hope to find a publisher in Venice for Timkins's journal; we also believe we will find a welcome from the local evil talking cat community. And if anyone had told me a few years ago that the paragraph I have just written would ever even make sense to me, I would have said they were insane.

I have written this quickly, and included such documents along the way as will, I hope, clarify and amplify. Personally, I am drawn, over and over, to the heartbreaking passage in Timkins's journal where he writes, 'I am to sail on the *Endeavour*! And I am but two years old!' I grieve for the noble Hodge, who tried to warn young Timkins; I grieve also for the kindly surgeon Mr Monkhouse, of whose existence I had never heard until about twelve hours ago. 'The cat be mine,' he said so simply. 'The cat be mine.' Like Timkins, I am thoroughly dismayed by Captain Cook's offhand account of his surgeon's death at Batavia; but then, apart from using a swear word in an unacceptable manner, Cook himself scarcely appears in this narrative at all, and it occurs to me now (belatedly) that I wasted quite a lot of time reading up on him.

Before they went to sleep, everyone contributed something, to help draw this account together – Roger, Mr Nolly, Wiggy, and even, of course, Mrs Fletcher, who possessed the photocopy of Tetty's Devil's Appointment Request form. Wiggy's much-mentioned *Endeavour* screenplay fragment failed to find a place in the narrative, so I shall bolt it on the end, because he'll be furious with me otherwise.

If there is anything else missing from this hastily compiled chronicle, I apologise. There is still so much to know about Roger. Who rescued him from the well? What is his 'weak spot', as so darkly referred to by Tetty? Meanwhile, my own curiosity still demands to know how exactly Timkins kept his journal (i.e. how did he write it?), but my questions evidently trespass on the most sacred of all cat secrets: they have made it clear to me that I must not ask. Obviously these cats can read the printed word, but when the Lunar cats make their notes, they do not hold pen to paper: they make secret little scratches – something like the ancient script of cuneiform. Naturally, I fear to ask Roger directly if cats were responsible for inventing cuneiform. I wouldn't put it past him to say that he and the Captain were once great friends in Syria with the cat who wrote the *Epic of Gilgamesh*.

It has been interesting to stay awake on a sleeper train through France, by the way. Normally one spends these night-time rail journeys waking up every couple of hours and peering through the smelly curtains to see station signs that make no sense. Are we going in circles? you think. How long have we been sitting in this siding? But then, in the morning, finding oneself in the right location, one forgets the suspicions of the night. Well, I can now attest, having been awake right through the small hours, that the train does indeed shunt sideways, loop round Paris three times, rattle and stop, reverse up the track for fifty miles, sway from side to side just for the hell of it, and then stop for a raucous chat with some other trains in the middle of nowhere before pulling itself together and covering the track to Nice at breakneck speed to make up for all the lost time.

I had not been considering a Christmas trip to Venice. I had been considering something quite the opposite: collecting my little dog, paying the vet, reading my emails, getting some festive shopping and resuming a quiet life with no evil talking cats in it. I was going to return all the library books in the New Year. I was going to attempt some tidying up. But I seem to have ended up with the opposite of my desires. The thing is, there was no alternative to flight. It is now 6.30 a.m. on Wednesday, 24 December. Tonight at midnight, at the full moon, Beelzebub will appear as requested at a small house in Bromley, and he will find no Tetty. He will find no Oviri. He will find no new

Cat Master. Finally, he will find no house. But he will, apparently, sift through the debris. I said to Roger, 'Perhaps he'll just let this go?' But Roger assures me that if there is one thing you can rely on with Beelzebub, it's that he does not let things go. Probably, his main ire will be directed at the absconded Tetty – which is a good thing for us, as it buys us time. According to the form she filled in, she has contracted half her immortal soul to him already; he will pursue her methodically, Roger says, until he attains the other half.

But among the debris, he will find the giveaway DNA of two innocent people – of Mrs Fletcher and myself. A glove with hair in it; a lavender bag with leg hair stuck to some adhesive tape. Roger says that if the Devil has been promised a new Cat Master, a new Cat Master is what he will want. Mrs Fletcher and I are fugitives from the Devil, and if it seems odd, in the circumstances, that I still know her only as 'Mrs Fletcher', that's just the way it is (although she did refer to herself as Lucy in a weak moment earlier, I couldn't help noticing).

We are well south by now. There is no sign of dawn. We will be in Venice by the afternoon – wintry but bright, perhaps. The low sun glittering on the Lido. We must remember to alert the local cats to the peaceful and uncompetitive purpose of this visit: it would be a shame if they deliberately burned down the Fenice Theatre again, just to show the Lunar cats what they can do. On the rack above, I hear little snores from the Lunar cats, for whom I already feel considerable affection. I am especially drawn to Mrs Stella – I will make it my personal cause to get her up to regular 12pt from the 10pt type size in which she has unfairly languished for so long. There is much to be learned from these Lunar cats, I feel; but there is also much I can teach them – such as how to get through doorways in a coordinated and dignified single file.

Watson presses his warm bottom against my thigh, and I shiver violently but do not wake him up. I stroke his tail. His tummy rises and falls, and he stretches his legs. From one of the open bags above Mrs Fletcher's head, I can see the wakeful eye of Roger studying me as I write.

'Just finishing,' I say softly.

'Get some sleep,' he says, with kindness.

'I'm putting Wiggy's screenplay at the end,' I said.

'You'll probably regret that.'

'I know.'

I shuffle my papers into final shape. I scratch my ankle and close my eyes.

'Happy Christmas, Roger,' I say.

For now, this is honestly the best that I can do.

BONUS FEATURE: WIGGY'S SCREENPLAY

Note from Alec: remember Wiggy wrote this when I was trying to establish whether Dr Johnson's cat Hodge had been on the *Endeavour,* and I had foolishly mentioned to Wiggy that the word 'sausage' does not appear in Johnson's *Dictionary.*

The cat HODGE *is up in the rigging of* CAPTAIN COOK'S Endeavour. *Wind whistles through the sails. The sea sparkles. Below, the young naturalist* JOSEPH BANKS *and his foreign scientist friend* SOLANDER *are sorting through some plants. Fronds everywhere.* HODGE *looks down. A condescending smile flits across his handsome feline face.*

JOSEPH BANKS

(*fed up*)

I just don't know what to call this one, Solander, do you? Look at it! Same old stalk. Same old fronds. Same old green colour. Pah. I've completely run out of ideas.

SOLANDER

(*accent of some kind*)

Ach. So haff I. We haff named zo many new plantz already!

CAPTAIN COOK *appears beside them.* HODGE *raises an eyebrow.*

CAPTAIN COOK

(*enquiringly*)

Problem?

SOLANDER

(*grumpy*)

Too right, *mein capitaine.*

COOK

Tell me. I am after all captain of this vessel, the *Endeavour.*

BANKS

Yes, you are.

COOK

And I am a kind man. It's true that I go nuts on the third voyage, which gets me killed by native Hawaiians, but at this stage I am quite reasonable, though a bit bluff in a forgivable Yorkshire kind of way. So, why the long faces?

BANKS

It's just – it's just having to come up with so many names! You've no idea what it's like, egad.

BANKS *angrily tosses botanical specimens about. In someone who will later be Top Chap at Kew Gardens (and President of the Royal Society, whatever that is), such childish behaviour is a bit shocking.*

COOK

(bitterly, with an audible 'ha!')

Ha!

BANKS

What do you mean – 'ha'?

COOK

I mean that I have no sympathy, young Mister Banks. Look at how many sodding names I have to come up with myself – day after sodding day, week after sodding week!

Close-up on HODGE *(in rigging).*

HODGE

(to himself)

And yet you never ask me for my help.

Back on deck.

SOLANDER

(to BANKS, *hotly, and evidently not for the first time)*

I haff told you over and over again to bring ze Johnson'z Dickssionary wizz us, Banks, but did you listen?

BANKS

Oh, not this again.

SOLANDER

But I did say—

BANKS

I know!

SOLANDER

And you wouldn't listen—

COOK

If only there was someone on this fucking ship who knew about fucking words!

The others react at such an outburst. COOK *begins to pace up and down. The others exchange glances.*

COOK

(*passion*)

Banks, I didn't tell you this, I was too embarrassed. But I nearly called an island 'Sausage Island' last week just because it was in the shape of a sausage!

The others gasp. We see a helpful aerial view of an island shaped exactly like a sausage.

BANKS

(*shocked*)

You never!

COOK

I did.

BANKS

You never!

SOLANDER

(foreign exclamation; check spelling later)

Ay corumba!

Flashback to dark interior of JOHNSON'S *house in London.* HODGE *sitting on a shelf in an upstairs room. On the wall behind is a double portrait of* JOHNSON *with the cat. Both look happy.*

JOHNSON

Hodge, help me with this, my darling kitty.
Which definition of 'sausage' do you prefer?

JOHNSON *puts three slips of paper in front of the cat, who reads them solemnly and then – with grave certainty – sweeps them all aside.*

JOHNSON

(confused)

What are you telling me, Hodge? You have to choose one.

HODGE *sweeps the slips off the shelf. They flutter to the floor.*

JOHNSON

I see.

JOHNSON *seems to understand, but then realises he doesn't.*

JOHNSON

No, I still don't understand.

HODGE

(*sarcastic; in a manly voice like Liam Neeson*)

Sausage? Really? I mean, come on.

JOHNSON

(*impressed*)

Bless you, Hodge. You're right! Sausage is a word quite unworthy of the dictionary!

He hugs HODGE *to his chest and offers him an opened oyster.* HODGE *rolls his eyes as if to say,* Not oysters again? *but graciously accepts, extending his attractive little pink tongue to lick up the living bivalve mollusc from a marine or brackish habitat.*

The Cat Master

Readers of *The Lunar Cats* will, I know, emerge from the experience with many pressing questions. For example, is the author of this book by any chance certifiably deranged? Is there a real-life model for the little dog Watson, and, if so, is he very lovely? But above all, was there a real Dr John Hawkesworth in the eighteenth century, whose fall from literary eminence was so calamitous that the bold supernatural explanation advanced in *The Lunar Cats* might actually seem to hold water? You will be delighted to discover that the answer to all of these questions is yes. The author is certainly unstable, the real-life dog is absolutely adorable, and John Hawkesworth was indeed the real – if obscure – chap who received £6,000 in the 1770s to author 'the voyages undertaken by the order of his present majesty for making discoveries in the Southern hemisphere'.

It may seem odd to be fascinated by the downfall of a man that almost no one has heard of. But for many years the fate of the real John Hawkesworth (1720–73) has lingered in my mind, as a starting point (at least) for a story. 'There is something in the return of Captain Cook from the first voyage,' I've been saying, boringly, for years. 'I feel there's something in the writing up of the journals.' Initially, I was just fascinated by the idea of an untravelled literary man having the nerve to tackle such an important and specialist topic. I understood well enough that journalism in the eighteenth century was, quite respectably, a branch of fiction: Dr Johnson famously composed highly admired parliamentary reports that he more or less made up. But with the *Voyages*, the distance between writer and subject seemed immense and daunting: on the one hand, the London hack bent alone over his desk in a candlelit room; on the other, the stout and crowded little ship *Endeavour* sheering through uncharted crystal seas. Did Dr Hawkesworth know what an azimuth was? What did he know about flying fish? Had he ever even seen a naval chart, let alone been the first person to map a coast on the far side of the world that ran for hundreds and hundreds of miles?

My first instinct with Hawkesworth, then, was to identify with him as someone overwhelmed by the task. Poor chap, I thought. Such pressure of expectation! The more I learned about him, however, the more this sympathetic identification failed to hold. 'Hawkesworth evidently endured success badly; his personality and character defects were intensified by his rise to public eminence,' says one modern historian. Or to put it another way: 'Hawkesworth is grown a coxcomb, and I have done with him,' as Dr Johnson said, with that thumping finality he was known for. The conclusion was soon inescapable: Hawkesworth's story turned out to embody a classic lesson in hubris – he was undone by pride. When he finally overreached himself, he plummeted into ignominy, obscurity and the grave. This is why his name is unfamiliar. Boswell barely mentioned him in his *Life of Johnson* (1791). The subsequent literary canon just ignored him. His sole biographer, John Lawrence Abbott, wrote in 1970 that John Hawkesworth 'did not leave a mark visible across the centuries'. It is a cliché to speak of a 'meteoric rise': for Hawkesworth, it was his hurtling and annihilating fall to earth that had most in common with a rock on fire.

The real Hawkesworth probably did not consort with Beelzebub, nor is there any evidence of his grooming a group of overeducated cats for evil purposes. But in most other respects, the account of Hawkesworth in *The Lunar Cats* is based on the facts. He began his literary career with the serious disadvantage of little classical learning (the title of 'Doctor' was honorary, conferred on him by the Archbishop of Canterbury in 1756). But he did possess talent – in particular, an ability to mimic the style of Johnson, whose friend he became in the 1740s. When Johnson stopped writing the parliamentary debates for the *Gentleman's Magazine*, Hawkesworth took over. It is true that in nearly every field of literary endeavour attempted by Johnson – Oriental tale, periodical journalism, stage play for David

Garrick – Hawkesworth followed the example, and reaped better financial rewards. It is also true that Johnson did not defend his former friend when he was under attack. However, my favourite piece of evidence concerning Johnson's feelings towards Hawkesworth comes in his essay on Swift in the *Lives of the English Poets* (1779–81):

> An Account of Dr. Swift has already been collected, with such diligence and acuteness, by Dr. Hawkesworth, according to a scheme which I laid before him in the intimacy of our friendship. I cannot, therefore, be expected to say much of a life concerning which I had long since communicated my thoughts to a man capable of dignifying his narration with so much elegance of language and force of sentiment.

What else is true about Hawkesworth in *The Lunar Cats*? As we learn from the painful exchange between Timkins and Hodge, Hawkesworth was comfortably married, and lived in Bromley in a fancy dwelling known as the Grete House. He was the literary editor of the *Gentleman's Magazine*; he also edited (and wrote many essays for) the periodical

The Adventurer. He also, as Hodge so uncharitably declares, never wrote a thing worth quoting. But he seems to have been good company, and it was his friendship with influential people (such as Charles Burney) that led to the huge commission from the Admiralty to write up the voyages to the South Seas. Incidentally, in *The Lunar Cats*, Alec and Roger are both wrong to assert that Hawkesworth received £6,000 for the commission; in fact, this was the sum he sold the rights for. The difference may seem unimportant, but I feel that in the envious moil of eighteenth-century Grub Street, the fact that Hawkesworth managed to sell his book for such an enormous sum (rather than receiving it as the going fee) would have made him all the more hated and despised.

Why did the *Voyages* get such a stinking reception when they were published? Had Hawkesworth done such a bad job? Why haven't the *Voyages* been seen, on the contrary, as a phenomenal feat of literary vicariousness (I believe he was never on a ship in his life) and also of editorial collation? A mere glance at the primary materials (as in the wildly varying accounts of the dunkings at the equator we see in *The Lunar Cats*) shows what a task it was for their editor to find even a simple narrative line. Meanwhile the two main sources – the journals of Banks and Cook – clash impossibly in terms of style and intent. But this is where the hubris comes in, because Hawkesworth's interesting solution to the problem was often not to choose between Cook and Banks, but a) to override both of them, and b) to fill in the gaps with his own stuff.

In terms of the book's readability, this authorial decision was probably a good one. The great Cook scholar J. C. Beaglehole, writing in 1963, summarised Hawkesworth's work as 'a classic not of English prose but of English adventure'. And it didn't hurt Cook at all that the received idea of him was for many generations taken straight from Hawkesworth: the editor's essayistic style misleadingly conferred on Cook spurious qualities of nobility and philosophical reflection. But whatever the eventual effect, Hawkesworth's degree of disrespect for the original, precious sources still smacks mainly of conceit. In a conversation with Boswell in 1776, Cook objected to Hawkesworth's practice of drawing 'a general conclusion from a particular fact' – in other words, of editorialising. Boswell agreed. He said, 'He has used your narrative as a London tavern keeper does wine. He has *brewed* it.'

He certainly paid the price. On publication, he was assailed from all quarters and accused of heinous faults. Writing fifty years later (in 1821) in an account of Kentish writers, Rowland Freeman still seems shocked by the animus that was turned on poor Hawkesworth: 'That much of this outcry proceeded from envy, and that execrable fondness for detraction so natural to bad men, which induces them to pursue merit as the fairest and noblest game, we have not the slightest doubt.'

But some of the complaints were not born of envy; they were genuine. Many readers were disappointed in the *Voyages* and felt short-changed when they discovered that (for their outlay of three guineas) those far-off exotic South Seas contained, not mythical giants and exciting sea monsters, but oversexed and bellicose indigenous people, a bit of coastline, and vast amounts of featureless salt water. Others objected to the shocking sexual laxity revealed in the sailors of His Majesty's Navy. None of this was Hawkesworth's fault: in fact, he had deliberately toned down the naughty bits. But the main objection was to the part of the book that was unarguably Hawkesworth's own: his grandiose preface. Here he completely overstepped the mark. Instead of declaring himself a mere humble conduit, insufficient to the task, never met a flying fish, et cetera, he used the opportunity to express his own misgivings on the use of firearms against defenceless savages in the cause of exploration, and then made an insane decision: he challenged Cook on theological grounds for his naming a passage of water (off the coast of modern-day Queensland) 'The Providential Channel'.

Rereading the preface yesterday, I found myself begging Hawkesworth to pause and rethink. 'Just don't go there!' I cried. 'Do not mention the Providential Channel! There is no need!' But of course he still did, although what provoked him to do it remains a mystery. One of the most dramatic events of the first voyage was when the *Endeavour* snagged on the Great Barrier Reef in August 1770 and looked set to capsize. In their journals, both Cook and Banks describe this near-disaster in vivid terms – especially how tight it was to get back through the reef to open sea. Cook notes that he decided to call their route the Providential Channel, but that is all he says; he makes nothing of it.

Banks doesn't mention the naming of the channel (perhaps he didn't know). There is no indication in either journal that anyone fell to their knees to thank God in particular on that day for saving them.

But in his preface, Hawkesworth decides to make an issue of it. Begging his readers to allow him his 'right of private judgment', he asks us to consider whether God really had anything to do with saving the *Endeavour* in this instance. God is surely present in all things, Hawkesworth says. Thus He was just as responsible for getting the ship on to the reef as He was for getting it off again:

> It is true that when the *Endeavour* was upon the rock off the coast of New Holland, the wind ceased, and that otherwise she would have been beaten to pieces; but either the subsiding of the wind was a natural event or not; if it was a natural event, providence is out of the question . . . If it was not a mere natural event, but produced by an extraordinary interposition, correcting a defect in the constitution of nature, tending to mischief, it will lie upon those who maintain

> the position to show why an extraordinary interposition did not take place rather to prevent the ship's striking, than to prevent her being beaten to pieces after she had struck.

To you and me, this argument might sound perfectly good (and well made), but it was evidently incendiary in 1773.

Did Hawkesworth really die as a result of critical attacks? It seems that he did. Accused variously of being grasping, boring, unreliable, lewd or unchristian (take your pick) – within months, he was gone, killed by his own book. His health had been undermined by the effort of working on the *Voyages*; he was also involved in legal cases. But it was the shock of his literary reversal that was surely the mortal blow. If the term 'backlash' had not yet been coined in 1773 (and I think not), it was suddenly urgently required. Anonymous critics joined together in a vicious and universal condemnation that feels very much like the trolling of today. 'You are *lawful game,* and ought to be hunted by every friend of virtue,' writes someone in the *Public Advertiser* in July 1773, who calls himself 'A Believer in the Particular as well as the General

Providence of God'. He goes on: 'You have verified the maxim that those who are destitute of the fundamental principles of religion and morality will grasp at gold with avidity, though it cannot be seized without injustice.'

So that is the real John Hawkesworth. I recommend John Lawrence Abbott's *John Hawkesworth: Eighteenth-Century Man of Letters,* and also an excellent essay on 'Hawkesworth's Alterations' by W. H. Pearson in the *Journal of Pacific History* (see bibliography, below). The big question remaining is obvious. After all he went through in his real life, does John Hawkesworth really deserve to be dragged from obscurity in the twenty-first century and reinvented as an evil Cat Master bent on wicked work? Didn't he suffer enough? All I can do is ask you to consider one thing: does it at least *fit the facts* that Hawkesworth was Cat Master from 1754 to 1773 and had a deal with Beelzebub for worldly success – a deal that went horribly wrong? The answer is yes. Yes, it does fit the facts; one might almost say it was designed to do so; moreover, the supernatural interpretation is so much more satisfying than the mundane one that it is frankly astonishing to me that no one has thought of it before.

And I'll tell you another mystery that is now explained. When modern historians painstakingly compare Hawkesworth's account of the voyages with those of Banks and Cook and scratch their heads over the philosophical passages that seem to have no authority to back them up – well, the reason for that is now, thanks to *The Lunar Cats,* as plain as day! We lucky insiders know of an *Endeavour* journal that no one else has ever seen, don't we? It is so good to think that perhaps Hawkesworth came a cropper because of using Timkins!

Lynne Truss
July 2016

Bibliography

Abbott, J. L., *John Hawkesworth: Eighteenth-Century Man of Letters* (University of Wisconsin Press, 1982)

——, 'John Hawkesworth: Friend of Samuel Johnson and Editor of Captain Cook's Voyages and of the Gentleman's Magazine', *Eighteenth-Century Studies*, vol. 3 (Spring, 1970)

Banks, J., *The Endeavour Journal of Joseph Banks 1768–1771*, ed. J. C. Beaglehole, two vols (Public Library of New South Wales and Angus & Robertson, 1962)

Cook, J., *The Journals of Captain Cook*, ed. Philip Edwards (Penguin, 1999)

Freeman, R., *Kentish Poets* (Canterbury, 1821)

Hawkesworth, J., *Almoran and Hamet* (1761), collected in Mack, R. L. (ed.), *Oriental Tales* (Oxford University Press, 1992)

——, *An Account of the Voyages Undertaken by the Order of His Present Majesty for Making Discoveries in the Southern Hemisphere*, three vols (Cambridge University Press, 2013 [1773])

Hawkesworth, J. with S. Johnson, R. Bathurst and J. Warton, *The Adventurer* (London, 1814; reprinted by Nabu Public Domain Reprints)

Parkinson, S., *Journal of a Voyage to the South Seas* (Caliban Books, 1984)

Pearson, W. H., 'Hawkesworth's Alterations', *Journal of Pacific History*, vol. 7 (1972)

Lynne Truss is the bestselling author of *Eats, Shoots and Leaves,* as well as a journalist, arts and book reviewer, sports columnist and regular broadcaster for BBC's Radio 4. She's had two plays performed at the Edinburgh Festival, including 'Hell's Bells' in 2012.

Her last novel, *Cat Out of Hell,* was published in 2014 and marked the unheard-of switch of allegiance from cats to dogs. *The Lunar Cats* reveals her new-found loyalty to be just as strong.